Dr. Kildare's™

Crisis

G·K
Hall
&Co.

**Also published in Large Print
from G.K. Hall by Max Brand™:**

The Bandit of the Black Hills
Calling Dr. Kildare™
Gun Gentlemen
Hunted Riders
The Nighthawk Trail
One Man Posse
The Rancher's Revenge
Ronicky Doone
Silvertip's Roundup
Smiling Charlie
Tragedy Trail
Valley of Vanishing Men
Western Tommy

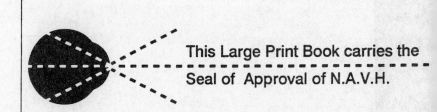

This Large Print Book carries the
Seal of Approval of N.A.V.H.

Dr. Kildare's™
Crisis

Max Brand™

G.K. Hall & Co.
Thorndike, Maine

Published in Large Print by arrangement with Golden West
Literary Agency.

G.K. Hall Large Print Book Series.

Printed on acid free paper in Great Britain.

Typeset in 16 pt. Plantin.

Library of Congress Cataloging-in-Publication Data

Brand, Max, 1892–1944.
  Dr. Kildare's crisis / Max Brand.
     p.   cm.
   ISBN 0-8161-5873-8 (alk. paper : lg. print)
   1. Physicians—United States—Fiction.   2. Large type
books.   I. Title.
[PS3511.A87D7   1994]
813′.52—dc20
                                                    93–21148
                                                       CIP

CONTENTS

CHAPTER ONE

MAN ON FIRE

Kildare came out of the operating room trundling Gillespie's wheel-chair and looking straight ahead to avoid some of the compliments; but he had to pause when old, great Dr. Ackers said: 'Good work, doctor. A fine pair of hands. Eleven minutes and twenty seconds from the first incision to the last stitch. We minimize shock, with speed like that ... And that was a bad kidney to get out ... I could use these hands, any day you're through with them, Gillespie.'

Gillespie drew together the formidable white brush of his eyebrows: 'Maybe you can have them damned soon, Ackers ... Get those useful hands off my chair, Kildare. They're too fine to be used like a nursemaid. You've taken plenty of my time, but I won't have you taking my exercise, also.'

He wheeled himself down the corridor with Kildare walking silently beside him.

'Speed, speed!' snorted Gillespie. 'No place to get to, and faster ways of getting there. That's the Twentieth Century, and be damned! And an old fool like Ackers praising it!'

'Was I too fast, sir?' asked Kildare.

'You know damned well you were too fast,' said the old man. 'What were you trying to do? Show off?'

There was a bit of silence.

'Well?' insisted Gillespie.

'Yes, sir. I was showing off—a little.'

'Leave speed for typists and airplanes; your job is to handle human lives.'

'Yes, sir. But I seemed to see my way right through that operation and—'

'Hold out your hand. Ha! Still a tremor in it, eh? Did you think you were crocheting, or what? ... Did you read that book on the lymph glands last night? What's the name of it?'

They were in the elevator, descending.

'Winslow and Parker wrote it, sir,' said Kildare.

'Well, did you read it last night?'

'No, sir.'

The elevator man's cheeks were swelling. Kildare, even from behind, knew the width of the grin on that face.

'No, sir, you didn't read it, eh? Wasn't time, I suppose?'

'There was an interesting pneumonia in Ward B, sir. I spent most of the night there.'

'Damn the interesting pneumonia. Nothing should interest you except what I tell you to do. You know that!'

'Yes, sir.'

'We've got to use our time the way misers

2

use money. There mustn't be any waste ...
What type was that pneumonia?'

'Thirty-one, sir.'

'Ah, was it? Complications?'

'A deep abdominal infection, sir.'

'Very pretty! Why didn't you call me?'

'You were sleeping, sir.'

'I wasn't. Had my eyes closed to rest them, that was all. I try not to waste my nights sleeping, Kildare. What made you think I was sleeping?'

'Your snoring, sir.'

'I wasn't snoring. I never snore. I may have been clearing my throat ... What did you do with the Type Thirty-one?'

*　　*　　*

They had left the elevator and were rolling into Gillespie's office. Kildare began: 'I used an injection of—'

'That's one of the manias today,' said Gillespie. 'Injections—injections—injections! How was the patient this morning?'

'All danger is gone now, sir, I believe.'

'Good boy!' said Gillespie. 'Damn the books and the theorists. Cures are what we want. What are you doing there?'

Kildare had taken from a small box two pills, which he now offered to Gillespie.

'I believe it's time for these, sir.'

'Pills—pills—pills!' roared Gillespie. 'You'll never make a doctor if you keep using pills. They're like sleep: chiefly a habit. The curse of the American people is the medicine cabinet in the bathroom. A hundred and thirty million people are putting pills in their mouths three times a day. How the devil can they amount to anything?

'There's no time left for continuity of thought or effort. A hundred and thirty million of the richest, healthiest people that ever lived, watching the clock and putting pills in their mouths. Take those damned things away!'

Kildare patiently kept offering them with a small glass of water.

'It's time for these, sir,' he insisted.

'How do I look to you, Jimmy?' asked the old man, anxiously.

'Not very badly, sir. How do you feel? Is the pain much worse this morning?'

'Questions—questions—questions!' shouted Gillespie. 'How are you going to make a diagnostician unless you start using your eyes? What difference does it make how people feel? A hundred million hours a day are wasted in this nation by people asking themselves how they feel. A mere habit and luxury of the mind.

'The question is: How *are* they, not how do they think they feel. Self-pity is ruining the white race, and you stand there and ask

4

me how I feel! ... I'm not so damned well, if you come right down to it, Jimmy.'

'You're a little worn, sir.'

'What should I do? Relax?'

'No, sir, you have to keep going.'

'Right! But what *should* I do?'

'Take these pills, sir, if you please.'

Gillespie, glowering, clapped them into his mouth and swallowed some water. He shuddered strongly.

'Superstition—witchcraft—good luck charms —they're all in a class with pills and pill-taking,' he declared.

Mary Lamont came in. The sun aslant through the window flashed on her white uniform as she went to Gillespie's desk and placed on it a small file of papers.

'Don't come in here without knocking, What's-your-name,' called Gillespie. 'Who told you to come into this room without knocking?'

'You did, doctor,' said the girl.

There was such young beauty in her that she always seemed to have been smiling and just about to smile again.

'I don't believe it,' said Gillespie. 'And why do you have so much starch in your uniform? So it will rustle? So people will know you're about? It makes you take up too much room. Don't try to take a place in the sun, around here.'

'No, doctor,' she said.

'Nurses are not human beings. They're merely pairs of hands for performing services—usually badly. And don't roll your eyes at Kildare, either. He only pretends about you. He doesn't take you seriously. For him, you're only a bit of simple diversion. A man has to have a little diversion, doesn't he?'

'Yes, doctor,' she said.

'The damned young idiot has been trying for speed records in the operating room, Mary,' said Gillespie. 'There's still a tremor in him. Take his hand and see. There! But wipe that fool look off your face. You're not seeing his immortal soul. Doctors don't have souls. But here's a young jackass who stays up all night nursing pneumonia patients and exhausting himself. What shall I do with him?'

'I might suggest a little diversion, sir.'

'You might suggest—What the devil are you talking about? He sees too *much* of you. Packmules lead an easier life than a man in love; their burdens have to be carried only part of the day; but this young fool has Mary Lamont in every breath he draws ... How many people in the waiting room?'

'Thirty-five, sir,' said the girl.

'I'll start taking them at once, sir,' said Kildare.

'You'll do nothing of the kind. Go into

your office and lie down for an hour.'

'But I have to write out a report on—'

'Damn the reports. Damn the writing. It might make a novelist out of you but it'll never make a doctor. Conover! Conover! Next patient, please!'

Kildare went into his adjoining office with the nurse behind him.

'He's been difficult? He's hurt you, Jimmy?' asked the girl.

'Gillespie? He never hurts me. But he's worse, Mary. He's failing fast. He's been dying all year. It isn't his body that the cancer's eating. It's his nerves; it's his soul. I've been watching the pain at work in his eyes and it makes me a little sick.'

'I know,' said Mary Lamont.

'He's a great man; and some day I've got to see him fall.'

'I know,' she repeated. 'Poor Jimmy! I think he would have died months ago, except that he loves you, and he has to last long enough to teach you everything he knows.'

'Everything?' Kildare laughed briefly.

'Is it true that you were up again, all last night?' she asked.

He shrugged his shoulders.

'Take some time off, Mary,' said Kildare. 'I've got to dig out some work now.'

'You'd better rest, hadn't you? Hadn't you better do what Doctor Gillespie suggests?'

'I'll rest when he goes.'

'Jimmy! You know he doesn't sleep any more than a bird.'

'I can stand it as well as he does. Lock the door when you go out. I'm not seeing anyone. Not a soul.'

A knock came at the door then—two quick taps, a pause, and three more. Mary frowned.

'That's Joe Weyman,' she said. 'Of course I'll tell him that you're not seeing anyone?'

'Joe? Of course I have to see him. He's an exception.'

'Everybody who wants your time— everybody's an exception, except me,' she said.

'Well—Let Joe come in,' he answered.

She paused an instant to look at the youth in his face and the weary age around his eyes. All of his features would follow that pattern before very long. He was one of the few who must find their happiness in labor; they accept the curse of Adam as a blessing.

Certainly *she* was not one of the elect who reach pain always, and fame once in ten thousand instances. Already he was at his desk, breaking down a pile of charts and picking up a pen to assemble statistics.

She went to the door and opened it on the wide shoulders and the barbarous grin of Joe Weyman, the ambulance driver. The apes in the trees seemed nearer kin to Weyman than young Dr. Kildare, and yet he made a place in his heart for the burly fellow.

'The doctor is *very* busy, Joe,' she said.

'Sure he is,' said Weyman, 'but I'm sick is why I wanta see him.'

'Come in, Joe,' said Kildare.

Weyman stepped inside. He looked from the doctor to the girl.

'He wants to see me alone,' said Kildare, already smiling a welcome to the ambulance man.

'All right,' sighed Mary, and went out, saying over her shoulder: 'May I have a word with you later?'

'Yes. Later,' said Kildare, as the door closed behind her.

'Not a little short with her, doc, are you?' asked Weyman.

'Short? With Mary? We understand each other,' said Kildare.

'Sure,' said Weyman. 'But they do the understanding and we do the guessing, usually ... Doc, I'm kind of low. I wondered could you give me a pick-me-up.'

'You've been hitting it pretty hard, Joe?'

'Hard? I hardly never hit it hard.'

'You were at it last night?'

'How would you guess that?'

'It's not too hard. You've got the blear in your eye and the thickness in your lip. You've been hitting it hard for a couple of weeks.'

'It's the job, doc,' said Weyman, slowly.

'You sit still as a stone waiting for a call; and then all at once it comes and you've gotta make tracks. Somebody's dying, somewhere. You gotta be there sudden. You go on the jump; you pick up some mug; you jump him back to the hospital; and then you're sitting still as a stone again, waiting for things to happen. It kind of gets on your nerves.'

'So you hit the hooch?'

'After hours, doc. Nobody never found nothing on my breath during hours. So I wondered if you'd give me a pick-me-up.'

'No,' said Kildare.

Weyman stared. He even moved a step closer, still staring, to make out that it really was Kildare who had made this strange response.

Kildare explained, carefully: 'I've watched the way you've been driving, lately. You're depending on the siren to cut your way through the traffic. And you're going to smash up, Joe. Some day with rain on the street. You'll go like a light. A side-swipe, and you'll be out.'

'Yeah. Maybe. But today—'

'I don't want you to feel any better. I want you to be as sick as a dog all day. It'll make you think until you realize that you've got to get out of this business. You've got to quit the ambulance job, Joe. Do something about it today. Will you?'

'You mean that I get nothing?' said

10

Weyman.

'Not a thing.'

Weyman turned clumsily towards the door. When he reached it, he laughed suddenly and looked over his shoulder.

'What d'ya think, doc?' he asked. 'I was almost sore at you!'

He went out, and Kildare looked after him for a moment, glancing into his life and his future and seeing the dullness of the hospital life without the bright little eyes and the broad mug of Weyman to enliven it.

That picture faded into other things: long rows of white cots, and the whisper of padding feet in the corridors; loaded wheel stretchers passing soundlessly; the glimmer of test-tubes in the laboratory, and the voice of Gillespie at work in his inner ear, constantly.

He turned back to his work, which was to relate all the complicated points of a high stack of charts. It meant multiplying, dividing, adding, correlating constantly. As usual, the moment he was employed, time ceased.

The day was not for him a series of little compartments into which he closed his attention for a few moments at a time; it was the sweep of a river that carried him with it, blindly. It was what Gillespie called 'the divine absorption.' Without it, he would have been an excellent doctor with a keen gift for diagnosis; with it, he gave promise of becoming the great thing that Gillespie had in mind as his destiny.

He was lost in his work; the voice of the city died out of his ears; there was no sound from the hospital, for him; before his mind's eye there began to grow dimly the foresight and the insight into a solution of his problem, a solution that was founded upon assembled hundreds of temperatures, blood-pressures, nerve reactions, contracting pupils.

'Jimmy, when you think you may be free ...' said the voice of Mary Lamont.

He withdrew only a step from the center of his dream.

'Don't bother me!' he said.

The door closed softly, a moment later.

'You've hurt her, this time,' said Gillespie.

That voice, as always, rallied him instantly from all of his preoccupation.

'How did you get in here?' he asked, turning bewildered toward his chief.

'How do you think?' asked Gillespie. 'I kicked the door open and wheeled myself in, and cleared my throat a couple of times; but you were out wool-gathering, asleep at your post.'

'I wasn't asleep,' said Kildare.

'I used to be able to do it,' said Gillespie, enviously. 'When I was your age, I could lose myself in a medical problem for days at a time. But now I'm old and fidgety and all I can do is try to remember. I'm too old to learn. But one thing I know without thinking: a man can't talk to a young girl the way you spoke to Mary, just now.'

Kildare stretched and yawned. His eyes sought the charts again.

'Don't be bored when *I'm* talking to you,' roared Gillespie. 'You think you own her because you're engaged to her? You think those eyes of hers don't see *other* men in the world?'

'Let her see them,' said Kildare. 'I haven't time to bother—and she knows it.'

'Does she, eh? I'll tell you what she knows. That she won't speak to you again the whole long day.'

'Nonsense,' said Kildare.

'You know better than I do, I suppose? I *saw* the way her head bent when she went out through that door. She's out there crying her eyes out, now. You're going to cut her out of your life, young Dr. Kildare; and when she's gone, where will you get another like her?'

Kildare yawned again, heartily.

'Not concerned, eh?' asked Gillespie.

'No, sir,' said Kildare. 'But I'd like to ask you about this second batch of charts on the—'

'Damn the charts. I'm talking about the happiness of your immortal soul—because the only soul in your damned life is going to be represented by that girl—and why do you think she left the room with her head bowed?'

'She was thinking of something she could do for me,' said Kildare, indifferently.

'Of all the confounded, pig-headed, brass-knuckled stupidity I've ever run into,' said Gillespie. 'Of all the damned flat-faced self-assurance...'

Here the door opened on Mary, who came smiling in and placed a slide-rule beside Kildare.

'Do you know how to run this, Jimmy?' she asked.

'Why the devil didn't I think of a slide-rule before?' sighed Kildare.

'And that's all the thanks he gives her,' groaned Gillespie, and wheeled his chair suddenly out of the room. Kildare looked up at the girl.

'What are you waiting for, Mary?' he asked.

'Not for thanks,' she said.

He smiled, faintly, and touched her with a quick gesture. He was beginning to be fully aware of her, something he rarely permitted himself during the course of working hours because once his mind set toward her it remained on that course for a long time.

'You have news of some sort,' he said.

'What makes you think so?'

'You've got lights in your eyes. Like fish in a creek. What's it all about?'

'Douglas is in New York.'

'What Douglas?'

'My brother. I've just seen him. Jimmy, he's a new man. He's tremendous. He has a great idea. He has the most glorious idea. That's what's in my eyes—what he's been telling me.'

'Right up on his toes?'

'Yes, like a wildcat.'

'I thought your brother Douglas was a slow fellow, a methodical chap, a sort of a measuring worm crawling along through his economics classes, and all that.'

'He was. But now he has an idea that sets him on fire. There's something you can do for him. Will you?'

'No,' said Kildare.

'Jimmy!'

'I don't like people who get on fire, all at once. I don't like the ideas that light them up, either. Not usually.'

'I'll tell him to come when he can,' said Mary. 'And you'll be simply dizzy when you hear him.'

'What's he going to do? Save the country?' asked Kildare.

'How did you guess?' she said.

CHAPTER TWO

BRAVE NEW WORLD

Lamont called at the hospital that afternoon and Mary brought him into Kildare's office. He was in his thirties, ten or twelve years older than Mary. He had gray hair, a pure and shining white around the temples, so that his gathered brows were doubly dark.

He had a starved body, inadequate to the bearing of burdens, and eyes from which the light had been burned out. There was no token of the man on fire whom she had described to Kildare. Mary was anxious about him.

'This horrible New York!' she said. 'See what it's done to poor Douglas in a day. He was on his toes yesterday; and now he's done in. What's wrong with him, Jimmy?'

Kildare looked at her again. She was dressed for the street and had on a pill-box hat that made her look as silly as a female hussar. She wore a string of thin beads that supported at her throat a pendant of deep blue lapis, threaded with golden veinings; and as she turned between Kildare and her brother the pendant swung excitedly back and forth.

'Young Doctor Kildare is the miracle

man?' asked Douglas Lamont. 'He can read our secrets at a glance? ... I'll sit down a moment, if I may.'

He slumped into a chair and dropped his head against the back of it.

'What *is* wrong with him?' Mary Lamont repeated.

'He's sleeping badly,' said Kildare.

'I put in eight hours, last night,' said Lamont, yawning.

'And woke up feeling as if you'd been climbing mountains all night?' asked Kildare.

Lamont was vaguely amused.

'These practical men; these practical scientists!' he said. He shook his head. Practical science was not important in his world, it seemed.

'Tell him really how you feel,' insisted the girl.

'Shall I?' asked Lamont, yawning again.

His head dropped still farther back. He stared straight before him with a sudden relaxing of all the muscles of his face and his eyes were utterly emptied, like colored glass from which sparkling water has been poured. It was the perfect picture of a man who has gone to sleep while he talks; there was even the loosening of the mouth, and there was something else about the picture that Kildare felt but could not note down, for all his quick diagnostician's eye.

'You really ought to give him a pick-up of some sort,' said Mary Lamont.

Her brother sat up and shrugged his shoulders. He seemed startled and thoroughly roused.

'No pick-ups; I'm not one for drugs,' he said, briskly.

'But it won't hurt you; it won't be habit forming; it won't be really a drug at all; just a sort of bracer, Douglas,' she urged.

'Nonsense,' said Lamont. He took a quick, deep breath. 'A man simply has to pull himself together, now and then. Make an effort of the will. That's all. I'm myself again, now. I had to father her for a few years,' he explained to Kildare, 'and now she thinks that it's her turn to mother me ... Shall we go along, Mary?'

'Why, have you forgotten everything?' she asked.

'Forgotten what?' snapped Lamont.

He was entirely changed, alert, and ready. Limp linen is not more changed by starch than this man had been changed by a single effort of the will. The temper had been put back into the steel, it seemed. 'There was the introduction, you know,' said Mary.

'I can't ask him to introduce something he doesn't know about,' said Lamont. 'Can you spare ten minutes, doctor?'

'I can,' said Kildare.

'You keep watching me,' said Lamont. 'Is

18

there something odd about me? Something medically curious?'

'Yes,' said Kildare.

'What, please?'

'I don't know,' said Kildare.

'Odd,' said Lamont. 'You see something, and you don't know what?'

'That's it,' answered Kildare, gravely. 'Forget about it.'

'Gladly,' said Lamont.

'You see, dear,' Mary explained to her brother, 'a diagnostician with a gift like Jimmy's only guesses, at first ... Jimmy, it isn't anything serious, is it?'

'I hope not,' answered Kildare, with the vacant eyes of a man who searches a crowded memory.

'This is being a little too mysterious, isn't it?' asked Lamont.

'Hush!' cautioned the girl, lifting her hand to silence her brother and looking with frightened attention into the vacant eyes of Kildare. 'Let him have a chance to think.'

'The fact is,' said Lamont, 'that my own health is pretty good. I have some bad dreams—like Hamlet. That's all. But let's drop the inquiry into my symptoms, doctor. Do you mind?'

Kildare returned slowly from his inward search.

'Not at all,' he agreed.

But he kept on watching Douglas Lamont

with a curious concentration which Mary had seen often before. She dreaded, now, what that narrowed vision might discover, almost as if a detective had been probing toward family secrets.

It seemed to her that a strain of conflict had been created between the two. There was something sharp, self-confident, irascible about Douglas which, she was sure, would arouse the antagonism of Jimmy Kildare.

She had hoped to make of them a single united force to accomplish her brother's purpose. So she looked anxiously back and forth from one to the other. The world of men and their preoccupations, not for the first time, seemed to her something fenced away behind a very high wall.

'May I talk?' asked Douglas Lamont briefly.

'Of course,' said Kildare.

'Let's forget about ourselves and think of the whole nation,' said Lamont. 'The whole three million square miles. A few cities dotted down here and there—and tens of millions of wasted acres.'

He paused, intent on Kildare.

'I'm seeing it,' agreed Kildare.

'Now that you have the picture in mind, I want you to think of something else: the billions of hours of waste time, the leisure of our hundred and thirty millions. Spare hours that could fertilize the useless land.'

'As the peasants do in Europe, you know,' suggested Mary.

'You're going to teach people to like work?' asked Kildare, smiling a little.

'Hush, Jimmy!' the girl cautioned him. 'It's really tremendous. Just listen and see!'

'Technology produces two things,' said Douglas Lamont, 'and these are cheap goods and leisure. But those leisure hours are the things that eat out the heart of the nation. Cocktail bars, silly radio entertainments, foolish movies, swing music eat up the leisure that ought to be a man's treasure.

'Our children grow up brainless because they grow up handless. Tempt them to use their hands and their minds will grow at the same time. They must learn to play and their play must make sense. The greatest game in the world is the building game. The greatest joy is to make things grow—anything: a house, a crop of vegetables.

'And half our children have concrete instead of soil underfoot. And the minds of half of our working men are decaying with too much leisure, or with the mechanical tending of mechanical machines. Are you listening, Jimmy?'

'No one could help listening.'

For in fact it was not the words that impressed him so much as the passion in the voice of Lamont, and the vision in his eyes

21

that already had foreseen a happy nation.

'The automobile expands our cities,' said Lamont, 'but not far enough. It gives working men burdens, not opportunities. It gives him a foolish patch of lawn to cut on Sundays, and a back yard where he can throw tin cans, and pick them up again. The soil is not temptation to him; and we must *make* the soil the temptation.

'Now follow me. From the great cities not jolting subway cars, but streamlined underground trains slide the tens of thousands, the hundreds of thousands of working people at the end of the day—not into cramped little suburbs, where the houses rub shoulders and one crying child can keep twenty families awake, but out into the real country, sliding the crowds along at seventy miles an hour. And at the end of the line the worker finds not a town but a small farm. A three or four acre farm.'

'A nation of small farmers?' asked Kildare.

'You see, Jimmy?' demanded Mary Lamont, happily.

'I partly see and I partly hope,' said Kildare.

'But how will millions of workers learn to spend their leisure farming? Who will teach 'em and how?'

'You see what they could do if they *were* taught?' asked Lamont.

'There's enough leisure in any family,'

22

agreed Kildare, 'to make three or four acres bloom from end to end.'

'Intensive cultivation,' added Lamont. 'There's no such thing as barren land in Italy because people work on every inch of the soil. Why, we'd have orchards with vegetables growing between the rows, and corn standing higher than your head, and potatoes, all the important vegetables as a matter of course, berry patches, alfalfa giving a couple or more heavy crops a year and fed to cows, and there would be sheep, goats, swine.

'An acre easily can feed one man; much more than feed one man if it's used properly. You can get three thousand pounds of wheat from one acre. You begin to see?'

'Millions of people growing most of their own food and getting healthy and happy while they do it?' asked Kildare.

'That's it. But think what happens in the beginning. Let's say we consider a man out of work, unlikely to find work again soon, and with a family on his hands.'

Kildare sat forward.

'Oh, that's it,' he said. 'Let's hear about the unemployed.'

Mary Lamont, instantly aware of the new attitude, smiled and nodded at him with approval. And yet from the first she had been assured and simply waiting for the magic of her brother to take effect upon Kildare.

23

Kildare added: 'I suppose that's about the toughest thing there is in the world: a sick man, let's say, out of work and with a family on his hands. Relief administrations are not enough.'

'You see that, do you?' snapped Lamont.

'Relief rots away the soul of a man, of course,' said Kildare.

Lamont laughed; there was a bright excitement in him that did not fade.

'My dear Jimmy, you're almost one of us,' he said. 'Let's take your sick man and his family. They are assigned to four acres, in the middle of which there is not a real home but the nucleus of one, something that will grow.

'The project offers the land and the house for no down payments; nothing will be asked for at least a year. There is also credit extended to the new man in the community center. There you find the store, the playhouse, the swimming pool and courts for games. It is not too far away for walking.

'In the community center there is the farm adviser, the mechanic-plumber, the electrician, the doctor, the carpenter—the few minds that are necessary to show this man how to use his spare time, how to employ his hands.

'He begins to plant his soil. He is told what crops will do best for marketing, what will best fill the family larder for the year. At

24

the same time, he is shown how he can expand the nucleus of his home—how the single room gradually can be expanded into a comfortable house.

'There is a need for some experience in construction. So the sheds are built first, the sheds to hold wood, and hay for the animals, for there must be animals. It is part of the natural economy. He cannot afford to buy mature animals, but the new-born ones cost almost nothing.

'With the sheds built against the coming of winter he can turn his attention to the expansion of his house. The passion to create is in him, now. In three months, we discover, the most ignorant and handless slum dweller will begin to react to opportunities for expressing himself in a new physical environment.'

'You've checked that sort of thing? You *know* how people respond?' asked Kildare.

'What have I been doing for years,' said Lamont, 'except examine the effects of reparation to the soil? But there never has been a scheme as large as mine, nothing that offered half so much real implementing of the idea.

'The beauty of it, you see, is the small scale on which it commences. The worker is not tempted to laziness by having comfort poured into his hands. Instead, a spur is stuck in his side; he sees security just ahead of him, if only he will make an effort toward it; and therefore he starts making the effort.

'His clumsiness does not shame him. Other men are going through the same phase. The whole community is aware of the novelty of its nature. It begins to take pride. The clever fellows are imitated by the dull ones. Stupid women become good cooks, watching the intelligent housekeepers.

'There will be no inertia, because there is no inertia in a new world, a frontier settlement; and it is a new frontier which we are creating. We are bringing the challenges of space and soil to the doors of the cities.

'And remember, again, the Kingdom of God is in the muscles; the work done by the hands informs the mind. These unemployed people, or day laborers, begin to awaken. They look up. Not toward wealth but toward culture.

'The greatest virtues, as thrift, cleanliness, industry, must grow among them because otherwise existence is impossible. As the small New England farms produced the strongest of our generations, so these little holdings will create another American race, rich in the strength of the soil.'

Lamont paused for only a moment, to look searchingly at Mary and Kildare. Seeing them intent, fascinated, he plunged on. 'The shadow, the dirt, the noise of the city is taken from these people. They cannot help

26

reaching up into the light.

'And at last even the unhappy necessities of technology, the brain-cramping needs of the machine, will not be able to destroy their spirits because every day the man and his family will be refreshed by the return to the soil.

'From charges on the state, they become taxpayers. Political machines cannot work effectively in such wide spaces. A decent political consciousness awakes and is schooled.

'In the end we may have a people tempted not by wealth but by the full vigorous life that springs out of the soil. The idle hours in which every corruption enters the soul and breeds will be stripped away.

'There will be employment for every hand, and on such small holdings the work of every hand can be seen and appreciated. There will be in these people the secure content of filled barns and crowded larders; they will have the interest of barnyard animals; instead of dirty pennies and store candy and vacuous radio programs and the insipid bathos of the moving picture, the children will be filled with excitement by the most fascinating of all moving pictures—the growth from the soil.

'They cannot be indifferent to seeds their own hands have planted and watered and fertilized. Every inch of every acre will bloom

27

and our country will return to the normal, true, strong way of life. Eyes will be sharpened, ears will be opened, and poetry will have a new birth!

'The communal consciousness develops into the national consciousness and these in turn cannot help but produce in the end the consciousness of a higher self.'

CHAPTER THREE

THE SICK SALESMAN

When he had ended, the thought still worked for a silent moment in the mind of Kildare while Lamont walked in continued excitement up and down the room. Mary could not stay in her chair.

'It must be heard by people who can do something about it,' she said. '*You're* convinced, Jimmy, aren't you?'

Kildare nodded, remembering suddenly the relaxation, as of sudden sleep, which he had seen overwhelm Douglas Lamont.

'I think it might work,' he said, 'with a man like your brother to drive it along and hypnotize any opposition. If he could last out the work until it's established...'

He considered the fragile body, the pale face of Lamont.

28

'Who *could* be opposed to us?' asked Lamont.

'Plenty of people.' said Kildare. 'Politicians who can't get a spoon into this bowl of soup. Newspapers who need something to laugh at. And all reformers who have their own special panaceas to apply. Your plan is too simple to be convincing—unless you're on hand to do the talking.'

'And who'll keep me from being on hand?' asked Lamont.

'You're not terribly strong, you know,' said Kildare.

'I have strength for this, though,' said Lamont. 'I tell you, Jimmy, I could use myself up to the last ounce, and the final bit of me would still throw a light for the fools to see by. I have strength enough.

'I tell you, God wouldn't let me be consumed before I've put one sample, one pattern project on the map. I know a tract in Jersey where the land is cheap as dirt. It would be a reclamation project for both men and acres. Nothing lost. Everything gained.'

'But he has to have money,' said Mary Lamont, 'and that's why I thought of you. You know Paul Messenger. He'd *have* to listen to anyone you send to him.'

'That *would* be good,' said Lamont. 'I've heard of the Messenger millions.'

'The trouble is,' said Kildare, studying the

starved body of Lamont again, 'that I'm not an economist like you, Douglas. I can't pretend to be a sound critic of ideas like yours. And Messenger is a great-hearted man. He'd give money; he'd give blood for anything that seemed right. And if I introduce you—'

'I see how it is,' broke in Lamont, coldly angry. 'Let's waste no more time on it. Glad I've seen you, Jimmy. Shall we get along, Mary?'

'Don't be sour about it, please,' said Kildare. 'You see, I've happened to do a few things for Mr. Messenger that he considers important. He'd take a recommendation from me almost—well, almost as an order. And I can't pretend to be an expert in economics, so that—'

'Jimmy, Jimmy,' exclaimed Mary, impatiently, 'you're not an expert in economics but Douglas *is*. How could he possibly be wrong about this when he's given his whole life to the study of—'

'Don't argue, Mary,' said Lamont. 'There's more than one rich man in New York. I wouldn't have Jimmy talk against his conscience.'

'I suppose it *is* right for me to telephone to Messenger,' decided Kildare. He tried to drive away his own reluctance. In the Utopia which Lamont had sketched it was true that he had not been able to pick flaws; and yet

30

the picture seemed a little too glowing to be true.

It was more than the scheme itself that troubled him. He could not drive from his mind the feeling that there was something pathologically wrong with this man, so wrong that he regretted the kinship with Mary.

Yet he found his hand reaching for the telephone. He could not resist the eye of the girl, bright with surprise at his delay.

He got the switchboard operator at the Messenger offices, the assistant secretary, then the secretary himself. That important man said: 'Impossible for Mr. Messenger to answer any calls just now. Give me your message, please.'

'This is Kildare. Will you ask...'

'Ah, Dr. Kildare?' came the hasty answer. 'I'll take a chance and put you through to him at once.'

And then Paul Messenger's strong, deep voice was saying: 'Hello Jimmy ... How are you, my boy? Nancy was asking about you yesterday, but you never let me have news of you to pass on.'

'I'm sorry to interrupt,' said Kildare.

'You're never interrupting. Not a thing in the world for me to do while you're on the phone.'

'The fact is that there's a friend of mine—a Douglas Lamont—who wants to talk to you. I wondered if you could see him before very long?'

'An old friend of yours, Jimmy?'

Kildare winced, but he knew that the strong voice of Messenger could be heard all through the office. He had to answer. 'A close friend of mine, as a matter of fact.'

'Of course I'll see him,' said Messenger. 'A close friend of yours, eh? I'll—wait a minute—I'll make myself free to see him. Send him over if he can come now.'

'That's kind of you,' said Kildare.

'Not kind at all. Shall I tell Nancy that you're well?'

'In fine shape, sir.'

'And that you're thinking of us now and then?'

'Of course.'

'Goodbye, Jimmy. Give us an evening when you can.'

'... That's decent of you,' said Lamont, still half offended. 'But I'm afraid that you've been dragged into this. I don't want to hitch you to what you feel is a lost cause, you know.'

'Nonsense, Douglas,' said the girl. 'Lost causes are the only ones that Jimmy likes.'

'Kildare! Kildare!' roared Gillespie from the next room.

He waved at the two Lamonts and hurried to his Chief.

Out on the street, Mary Lamont was for a taxi; her brother insisted on a bus. 'Extravagant,' he said.

'But it's a special occasion,' she urged. 'And it'll give you more time with Mr. Messenger.'

He grew solemn. He rarely was far from solemnity. 'Expenditure on the unessentials—if we could save that, we'd be able to fatten all our poor and dress them warmly,' he said. 'We have to be conscious of the whole social pattern; and we have to serve it all the time, Mary. You play with the idea now and then but it ought to be with us constantly.'

She smiled inwardly. There was no lightness about this good man. And in the old days he had been considered by many people a famous bore. How they would change their minds before long!

A thunderstorm rolled over Manhattan from the west. The rain slowed traffic; taxicabs thickened it like gruel in soup; the cross-town currents stalled between the great north-south avenues and started their horns in choruses of dissonance; but Douglas Lamont continued to talk, straining his voice so that other passengers in the bus became curiously aware of him.

With his starved hands he made gestures

which cherished the future of the commonwealth and the common man. People glanced at him smiling, with a touch of contempt; but when they overheard even a phrase they became serious.

His eloquence, Mary decided, lay not so much in words as in a radiation of earnestness. She herself was on the verge of smiling continually, moved by affection, pride, and that pity which we feel for people who are given utterly to any great and selfless cause.

When they came to the great building in which Messenger kept offices she said: 'I'll wait at the entrance for you, Douglas. Mr. Messenger is a big man, rather tense, good-hearted, but full of affairs. He loves Jimmy; he'll do anything for Jimmy; but all that he could do never would repay what Jimmy's done for him. However, I'd try to make your argument short, terribly short. You don't know how this New York pressure makes men cut their time into kindling wood.'

He listened to her, two-thirds of his attention already flowing forward, away from her. Then, with a hasty gesture of farewell, he hurried forward to an express elevator.

He looked small and hopelessly fragile in the crowd of office workers who were leaving the building. He leaned against the stream of them as if against the weight of a wind storm.

They went out, happy with the day's end, and he passed in, intent on their cause with a sacred concern.

Some day, she thought, his name would be so known and his face so familiar that all the unfortunate, all the downtrodden, all the unhappy people of the world would turn toward him as toward a light.

The elevator doors closed and he was gone from her sight. In the great hall of the building all sounds were subdued—the power-hum from the elevator shafts, the clicking of heels and the murmuring of voices—until the noise was like something in her own mind.

Through the crowd of hurrying office workers, mostly women, men moved singly or in small groups, at leisure that made them seem more important.

These were the lords of the land, the men of affairs, the owners and controllers. It was they who were almost bound to smile at schemes such as that of Douglas Lamont; and Paul Messenger was one of these. When she remembered this, her heart sank.

She went back to the street and stood against the concrete wall. The rain came in flurries and sudden strong gusts on the wind but she preferred the open because hope for her brother revived in that stirring air.

It was between day and night. The lower stories of buildings already were lighted; the upper reaches still had enough sunlight. She had an impression of the city as of an immense ship, voyaging and insecure.

After twenty minutes, she watched the entrance of the building carefully. At the end of half an hour, Douglas still had not appeared. She wondered, startled, whether he could have come down and out and gone away without seeing her.

But that would not be like him. He was full of calm, thorough method. Still anxiety led her back into the hall to watch the elevator doors opening, the passengers streaming out into the blue haze of the evening.

No doubt Douglas had been kept waiting. The interview itself could not have endured so long.

It was fifty minutes after he left her before she saw him again, walking beside big, handsome Paul Messenger. The rich man walked with his head lifted, his eyes straightforward, while Douglas Lamont hurried along half sidling as he turned towards his companion, still arguing—appealing vainly to an immovable figure, it seemed to the girl.

She was all at once cold with shame and hot with anger; but now as they drew nearer she was able to look more closely into Messenger's face and she saw that he was removed from her brother not by boredom and disdain but by the dream in which he was moving. The hypnotized, sleep-walker look was in his eyes.

She trailed after them. Even on the sidewalk her brother did not look about for her. He still was lost in his own talk as he climbed into Messenger's big car; and now they were gone in the traffic.

But she was not left alone. The certainty that Messenger had been entranced by the plan of her brother was ample reward and company for her. She only needed, now, someone to whom she could pour out her happiness.

There was Jimmy Kildare, of course. So she headed straight back to the hospital.

The whole ponderous mass of the Blair Hospital seemed unsubstantial to her as she entered it.

This work of Douglas, which eventually would take the millions back to the soil and the strength that comes out of it, must do away with a great part of our medical needs. Health comes with bending of the back. Out of such planning there must appear a mightier nation, simpler, less hurried, genially content with life.

She was walking in another century when she came to the waiting room of Gillespie with that famous sign in brass: *Dr. Leonard Gillespie. Office Hours: 12 a.m. to 12 a.m.* in token of his twenty-four hour day.

It was a miracle to find, as she did now, no more than half a dozen patients waiting. There was a tall woman with a sullen face and the clothes and manner of the great lady; there was a little Italian laborer, asleep in his chair; a scrawny boy sitting close to his mother; a Negress, huge with fat and dusty with fear; and an elderly man sleek with too many decades of good living—sleek, and soft, and rosy.

The girl said to Conover, the big Negro who presided over the waiting room: 'Is Doctor Kildare taking the line-up, or Doctor Gillespie?'

A dull roar came from behind the door, calling: 'Next patient!'

Conover smiled, for Gillespie had answered in his proper person. Mary Lamont crossed to Kildare's office and opened the door without knocking. That was his own request.

She was stepping in and closing the door behind her when the voice of Kildare stopped her, saying: 'I agree, Mr. Messenger. I think that *he* might put the thing through. But I'm not sure that he will have the strength to do it...

'I can't tell. It's simply that I guess at something pathologically wrong with him ... I'm only telling you this because I had to introduce him to you...

'No, no, I think he's the most honest man

38

in the world; but I'd like to have you submit his idea to a group of experts—experts in relief, housing, and all the things that he talks about...

'I'm glad you agree ... I don't know what's wrong. Nerves, perhaps...'

She stepped back from the room and closed the door soundlessly behind her.

CHAPTER FOUR

DIAGNOSIS DEFERRED

When Mary went into the Nurses' Home, she met Molly Cavendish about to go back on duty, looking always weary, always formidable.

The great Gillespie swore that she was the finest head nurse in history; she also was one of the most severe. There was no more delicacy in her than there is in a Missouri mule. Even into the private affairs of her nurses she pawed her way; because an unhappy nurse is apt to get absent-minded, said the Cavendish, and therefore she wished to know the minds of her nurses as well as she knew their faces.

Mary Lamont, remembering all the kindnesses she had received from this dour woman, smiled as she passed her on the stairs; but there was no smile left when she reached her room.

The bed tempted her. She wanted to throw herself face down on it; but it was necessary for her to attempt to think. So she sank into a straight-backed chair and let her thought return to the voice of Kildare, quiet, a little nasal, always grave, as he had said: 'I don't know what's wrong. Nerves, perhaps.'

'Nerves' is a word with a thousand meanings, including certain dreadful connotations from which her mind shrank away. Her eye automatically picked up the features of her room, in the meantime.

No social worker could have found anything wrong with it. It was an airy, clean, dry, substantial room with plenty of cubic yards of air space. The furniture was solid. Clearly it had been bought by someone who understood the wholesale world and how to get values.

On everything there was the sign of quantity production which saves us so many, many dollars. Not a thing in the room could give offense to anyone; and therefore there was nothing that could give pleasure, either.

It was a room like a gray day. Even if it had not faced north, sunshine would have been a stranger in it.

Mary Lamont could not have told why this room made her heart ache, because she was not a very logical thinker; but instinct had made her hang on the wall a warm Chinese print that opened the room like a window to the south. She looked now at the white crane that stood on one leg in the green water and among the brown rushes. They crossed and recrossed in a pattern that gave her quiet pleasure, always; but nothing gave pleasure, now.

She glanced at her shelf of books. She was not a great reader, it must be admitted. The gilt edges of her Bible had not been worn by much fingering and turning of the page.

Except for *Romeo and Juliet* and *The Tempest* and *Othello*, her one-volume copy of Shakespeare had sticky edges that never had been parted. She liked the famous love scene in the third act of *The Tempest*, except that Miranda was rather simple in giving everything away so quickly; and when she felt up to it, sometimes she read her *Othello* from the undressing scene with Emilia through the murder. It frightened and nauseated her; she was very glad and yet she was somewhat sorry, also, that modern man is not blown by such tempests of passion.

Beside the two famous books, she had some volumes of Lubbock which the man of her first love affair, some years before, had given to her. *The Chinese Clippers* and *The Colonial Clippers* and *The Log of the Cutty Sark* were not in themselves interesting to her; but she kept the books on the shelf

41

because they reminded her of the brown face of that sea-lover, and the finely incised lines about his eyes that came from squinting above the glare of the sunlit ocean.

She was proud that *The Way of All Flesh* was on the shelf and that she had read it through; because when she spoke of Earnest, serious, literate people were apt to look at her with new eyes. This pride led her to speak highly of Butler's grim book; but actually he made her shudder, he so leveled out life to a hateful monotony.

She had a few best sellers, though she wondered why they had to be so very long. There was also a battered copy of *The Prisoner of Zenda* which she kept defiantly on the shelf because she had adored it so much in her girlhood; and because she still hoped to meet some great, grave man with a red beard.

Of them all, two little thin, worn volumes of Katherine Mansfield were perhaps nearest to her heart. Mansfield made her determine to rub her eyes wide awake and begin to see things in detail; half a dozen times she had started a 'Journal' of her own, and though she never carried the effort beyond a few pages, the knowledge that the notebook was in the top bureau drawer was a comfort.

It enabled her to talk with an understanding sympathy when she met a writer; it made her confide to a friend, now and then, that if her life had been different—if there had been a chance really to live—if there had been just a *little* leisure—who knows?

As Mary faintly entered upon those old paths of thought, she was aware of something knocking on her mind like a hand at her door.

It was water dripping in the shower. She got up and jammed the lever so hard that she hurt her hand. The dripping stopped.

The physical pain gave her an odd relief. And as she came back into her room she saw Molly Cavendish standing in the open door. Something about her settled attitude showed that she had been there for minutes.

'Well, out with it,' said the Cavendish.

'There's nothing,' said Mary.

'That's a lie,' said Molly Cavendish. 'You're afraid because you've done something; or because something is about to be done.'

Mary went to her, smiling.

'I'm quite all right,' she said. 'It's sweet of you, but there's nothing wrong. Do come in.'

'Oh, shut up!' said the Cavendish.

'I'm sorry,' said Mary. 'I don't really know what you—'

'Stop this damned baby-talk and naivete,' said the head nurse. 'Something has scared you to death. What is it?'

43

'But not a thing has happened to me,' said Mary.

'To that lunk-head, Kildare, then?'

'Jimmy? No, he's as happy as his work lets him be.'

'And *you're* almost happy, too, you think you're lying so well. But you're not fooling me.'

She raised her big head and looked up towards that God who listens to impatient people. 'Those silly little brats!' she confided to His ear. 'The fact is,' she went on to Mary, 'that you're scared to death because you think I might find out what's in your mind.'

'No, Miss Cavendish. Of course not. There's not a thing that I wouldn't—and happily—not a thing—of course I'd tell you anything, and if I seem–'

'Bah! Stop gushing!' said Molly Cavendish. 'You'd talk to me as soon as you would to a mother, I suppose? All this damned sweetness doesn't melt in *my* mouth, Mary Lamont. I tell you, you're in such a dither that I wouldn't put you on a serious case. You're as full of jitters as a baby's rattle; and mind you, I won't stop till I've found out what it is!'

She slammed the door suddenly and left the loud echo inside the room with Mary. There was no other sound. Even the mournful voice of the city was lost, so that

Kildare's words came back to the girl more clearly than ever: 'I don't know what's wrong. Nerves perhaps.'

She began to sicken with fear again until a fine little glow of anger came to her rescue. She could remember her brother back almost to her infancy and there never had been a fellow of more steady and sober judgement. Of all the men she had known in the whole world, she told herself, there never had been one *more* sane than Douglas Lamont.

What about Jimmy himself, jousting at windmills, championing lost causes? What about the great Gillespie with his passions and ragings? There was nothing wrong with Douglas except the fire and light of a great idea.

But even as the thought passed through her mind, she began to grow cold with fear once more; for she knew that in Kildare there was the talent of the born diagnostician, sharpened to a needle-point by the training he received from Gillespie.

He had not come into his full power, to be sure, but he missed so rarely, so rarely! The whole hospital knew about him. Even among residents and internes there no longer was any jealousy. They were not shamed if they could not equal Kildare.

They looked up to him as to a genius; they pitied him because he was paying the price of devoted slavery which the genius always pays, his life subdued to his talent. And it was this Kildare who had seen something horribly wrong in Douglas.

She strained her attention and her memory of the scene between Douglas and Kildare. There was nothing strange about it. Douglas had been very sleepy until he warmed, suddenly, as a man of mind will do, to his theme.

And might it not be that Kildare, bighearted as he was, had been a little touched with jealousy when he saw her hanging so breathlessly on every word Douglas spoke?

It was at this moment, just as she was arguing herself back into a degree of confidence, that she remembered her grand-uncle, Peter Lamont. He was as thin as a wraith in her recollection, but it was a distorted wraith. The thought of some hereditary evil rushed on her.

She sat for a moment with her eyes tightly shut, then she got pen and paper and forced herself to write:

DEAR COUSIN CHARLES:
You know how things drop suddenly into a person's mind? Suddenly I've found myself thinking about our grand-uncle, Peter. All the Lamonts ought to know all about one another, but it seems to me that

no one ever speaks about Uncle Peter; and there's just a ghost of a memory that something horrible happened to him—and something went wrong with him before the end.

I remember a big man with wild hair and a tremendous voice, always shouting. Is that right? I remember him so clearly that all at once I simply *have* to find out what became of him. Do let me know. You're the family historian, you know.

Affectionately,
MARY

She sealed the letter. The taste of the mucilage lingered in her mouth until she forgot the cause of it. It became part of the strange dread that possessed her.

CHAPTER FIVE

THE GROWL OF KILDARE

Her telephone rang. The voice of Douglas said: 'Hello, Mary? Hello! Hello! ... Ah, there you are! Now, my dear, I've got something a bit ugly to say to you. But we always come clean with one another, we Lamonts, don't we?'

'Of course we do,' she said.

'What's the matter? You sound stifled? Have you been weeping?'

'No, Douglas; there's simply something wrong with the phone. *You* sound a little dim, too.'

'Do I? I don't feel dim. I feel damned bright and burning. Burned up, in fact!'

'Didn't it turn out well, Douglas? I saw you leave the building with Messenger and I thought he seemed so interested.'

'Did I walk right over you and never give you a look? Forgive me for that, Mary. I only remembered this minute that you were to wait for me there. But I had Messenger on the run and I couldn't think of anything else.'

'That's the only thing worth talking about. I *knew* that he was hypnotized. Oh, I'm so glad!'

'He *was* hypnotized. You know the rich; there's a decent impulse in them—a desire to give back what they've taken—a queer thing, partly good, partly merely for the sake of reputation—you know?'

'I know.'

'I lined out the idea as briskly as I could. I never felt better, Mary. The thing came rushing out, you see. It came out whole and entire, like a living birth. And that fellow has a fine eye, understanding, bright, a little impatient at first until I'd grabbed his interest.

'He took me home with him. I talked a good deal more. He wasn't bored. He was fascinated. God bless him. There's a noble fellow! I loved him for the way he listened.

'And it seemed to me that there was a way opening for all the laborers of America—all the poor of the world—all the unhappy devils who walk on concrete pavements instead of earth with life in it—it seemed to me that a way was opening for them to a real existence. And then—crash!'

'No, Douglas!'

'I tell you, I was at the top of the mountain, and now I'm almost at the bottom of the sea. I've not been thrown out, mind you. Everything still is courtesy and hope. But the heart's gone out of things. There's doubt, now, instead of faith. That's the acid that eats away the soul of a man. It's better to have faith in the devil than no faith at all.'

'Douglas, what's happened? You're so *terribly* violent.'

'I'll take hold of myself. It was this way: Mr. Messenger, when we got to his house, left word that we were not to be disturbed for anything, not even for an earthquake; then he took me into his private study. And the world was mine, Mary, until an interruption *did* come.'

'In spite of what Mr. Messenger–'

'There's someone more important than earthquakes in the Messenger house. You'll see. I had Messenger on the verge of writing *checks*! And then there was a knock at the door and a servant appeared. "I told you not to interrupt us!" says Messenger, very angry. The servant didn't bat an eye. He even smiled a little. "But this is Doctor Kildare on the telephone, sir," he says. You hear me, Mary?'

'I hear you,' she said, faintly.

That raging violence which was coming to her over the wire had still been bringing up the words of Kildare as she overheard them at his office: 'I don't know what's wrong; nerves, perhaps.'

'Well, this magic name of Kildare got Messenger right up and out of the room. He excused himself to me. He said: "There's one name that has taken precedence over everything else in this house." And he went out.

'When he came back, a long time later, he was a different man. The fire had gone out of him.'

'It may be, Douglas, that he'd simply escaped from the warmth of your argument. He wasn't seeing it all as clearly.'

'Nonsense. He couldn't have changed that fast if someone had not been working on him. He asked me to carry on with what I had been saying. But when I talked, I saw his heart was not in listening to me. Mind you, there was a queer way that Kildare had of looking at me, today.'

'No, no, Douglas!'

'I tell you, I saw it and I felt it. The man may love you, my dear, but he doesn't like your brother. Paul Messenger, five minutes after he came back from the telephone—and Jimmy Kildare—was standing up as a sign that I was through for the day. He was saying that after all he was, in spite of a great interest, by no means capable of pronouncing on a matter that needed the opinion of a sound economist and a welfare worker and someone who already had had experience in repatriating city labor back to the soil. He would arrange for a meeting between me and three or four men of that sort. He would have to depend on their judgement. Damn it all, Mary, what has Kildare against me? Why does he hate me?'

'He doesn't hate you, Douglas. There's no hatred in him. There's no cruelty or deceit in him.'

'Isn't there? I'm going to talk to him, face to face. I don't stab other people in the back, and I don't expect them to stab me.'

She cried out to him, but his receiver clanged hard on the hook.

I don't know what's wrong; the nerves, perhaps, Kildare had said.

And now, as she thought back upon her brother as she had known him, there was a great change between the calm, methodical

51

scientist and this man of fire, this impatient force, raging at restraints. A great change indeed—in the nerves, perhaps.

She gathered her strength like something that had fallen from her and left her in a naked weakness. After that, she left her room and went back to the hospital as fast as she could.

Whatever happened, she knew that she must keep this fire-new brother of hers away from Kildare, somewhat as she would have wished to keep wildcat away from bulldog. So she came hurrying once more into the waiting room of Gillespie and through it to the door of Kildare.

But there was no need for her to rap at the door. She could hear through it, not the words, but the voices: the high snarl of Douglas Lamont, and the deeper growl of Kildare.

CHAPTER SIX

SEE YOUR DOCTOR

To Kildare, the brother of Mary Lamont had claims to a humane and earnest consideration; but he was above all a sick man.

That was why he could not help regarding

Douglas Lamont with a professional eye; and the professional eye of a doctor, without mercy, kindness, or any human consideration, probes at the truth and nothing but the truth, which mind and spirit and body seem concerned only in hiding from him. So Kildare received Douglas Lamont, in spite of the best intentions, somewhat as a fencer receives an opponent on the point of a foil.

The head of Lamont, bowed as that of the scholar often is at the book-angle, was lifted now. He looked at Kildare with a fierce insistence saying; 'What is it, man? What's put you against me?'

'I'm not against you,' answered Kildare.

Lamont brushed protestations aside with a gesture of both hands.

'I can guess at a good deal of it,' he said. 'You and Mary want to be married one of these days. The result is that you're jealous of people who have an old hold on her. Isn't that it?'

'No,' said Kildare.

'Let's be frank,' argued Lamont. 'It's only human nature. A girl's past is the only thing about her that doesn't belong to her husband, eh? Even fathers and older brothers are damned nuisances. Aren't they?'

'I don't think so,' answered Kildare.

'Ah, but it isn't a matter of thinking, so much as instinct. You can't help being

53

against me; but let's have it out in the open. That's the best way, isn't it?'

'Of course, if there's anything to argue about.'

There was a sort of lifting and lightening of Lamont, a gathering of forces and then a repression of them.

'Why did you stab me in the back with Paul Messenger?' he asked.

'Stab you? In the back?'

'He was called to the telephone to talk to you. He was in my hand when he went from the room. He was out of my hand when he came back. What did you say to him?'

'I agreed with him that when you talk of your project you could set anyone on fire. I agreed with him that if you can stick out the job you're likely to put it through. But I told him that I thought you were a sick man.'

'Sick!' cried Lamont. 'A *sick* man? Take my pulse, my temperature. I tell you, I never felt half so well in my life. Well? Why, I'm lifted out of myself! If I'm ill, give the illness a name, my friend!'

'I can't do it,' said Kildare, still narrowing his eyes as he watched the other.

'In law,' said Lamont, 'a man is innocent until he's proven guilty. In medicine it seems that there's a different rule.'

His anger lifted his voice and gave an edge to it.

'I know how this seems to you,' said

Kildare, 'and I don't blame you for being angry. It's hard for me to explain to you. I have to carry with me a sort of blue-printed pattern of normality which means good health; and where there are variations, I feel them sometimes when I can't give them a definite name.'

'Do you mind telling me what it is that you *feel* about me?' asked Lamont.

'I feel that you're burning yourself up.'

'Burning myself up? Overworking, you mean?'

'No. Not the work. Right now you feel as if you could lift a mountain, don't you?'

'More or less.'

'Usually people don't have that sense of energy in their fingertips. Perhaps I sound like a stodgy fool; but usually men feel they can move the mountain that would break the giant's back—but only if they take it away a backload at a time.'

'It's because I have confidence. That's it, isn't it?'

'We all prefer to see confidence. It's like a success story. But you're on fire, Douglas. Even when you sleep you have dreams of millions of men and women persuaded and doing as you tell them to do.'

Lamont smiled a little at that and nodded; then plunged on with increased fervor.

'I have dreams of millions of happy people: the same poor devils whose

55

unhappiness I've seen in the day. Mind you, Jimmy, I've approached these problems the cold-blooded way. I've come at the social problems of economics through textbooks and then through grinding months of field work. I've heard dry professors talking and taken ten thousand pages of shorthand notes on them. I've laid a deep soil; but only recently a seed has germinated in that soil, and now the plant is growing, and it is going to be seen by the world.

'There's something in my heart and mind, Kildare, that is going to help millions. I don't want fame. I don't want glory. I'd rather do an anonymous job. But there are men and women as sound as oak who are turning into weeds because their hands are idle, and their brains are standing still, and therefore their souls are rotting in them!

'You talk to me about dreams? I still dream when I'm awake, and God pity the man who keeps those dreams from coming true.'

'I'll never try to balk them,' said Kildare.

'You will, and you do, and you *have* tried,' said Lamont. 'But why should I complain? I've made the truth shine in the eyes of Messenger, and I'll make it shine in the eyes of his experts, as he calls them. Damn the experts, I say. An expert is a book, not a man; his knowledge is a card index system. *You're* an expert, Kildare, and you're applying the cold poison of your remembered knowledge and your childish suspicion to me.

'But that's dull stuff compared with the thing that's in me. It's weeds compared with a cutting edge. And you, and all conservative thought like you, I'll mow down in my path and open a way to a new hope, a new chance for the stupid, the suffering, the inept, the soulweary!'

He changed, suddenly, from anger to compassion, and caught the hand of Kildare.

'Forgive me for being excited and angry,' he said. 'It seemed to me that since you love Mary you would have to love my plan. But I understand. Ordinary human nature revolts against high hopes and expectations. Everything important is a miracle until it's accomplished. I shall talk to you again, Jimmy. I shall lead you gently to a clearer understanding of what is bound to come. It cannot fail. I feel—I feel as if God had commissioned me!'

He left the room suddenly, without a farewell, and slammed the door to behind him.

Kildare moved to follow him, but instead he turned back to the diminishing stack of charts, and slide-rules, and the mass of figures which began to form a thick mist through which, very dimly, he was beginning to see the outlines of a destination, as one sees the loom and shadow of distant hills through a fog.

Long ago, in the days of his medical school studies when he was working his way through college, he had had to learn how to keep his two worlds of study and of outside work apart, perfecting that fine art of concentration which enables the mind to establish an exact focus and maintain it. Now he put the thought of Douglas Lamont aside, and with it all that exacting problem of the uncompleted diagnosis.

He grew aware, a little later, that someone else was in the room.

There was a soft rustling of papers, and then the crisp flickering of cards, all the sounds as quietly produced as possible.

That would be Mary, of course. She came vaguely into his consciousness, was dismissed; persistently returned, touching him like eyes that are fixed on the small of one's back. He dropped the chart-work from his mind and turned to her.

'What is it, Mary?' he asked.

She laughed a little.

'I'm getting the cards of the gout patients together,' she said. 'Dr. Gillespie wants them.'

He remained turned in his chair until she glanced at him.

'There's something wrong,' he said.

'Why, no,' she answered.

'You're worrying. It's about Douglas,' he told her.

'No. There's only a touch of a headache. That's all.'

'Look at me, will you?'

'Well?'

'You haven't a headache.'

'I have, though. Just a slight one behind the eyes.'

He glanced at his work, then rose reluctantly and gave her his full attention.

'I'm not going to be diagnosed, Jimmy,' she said, starting out of the room.

'Don't go; please,' said Kildare.

She turned at the door.

'Jimmy, don't be difficult,' she said.

'You're upset,' he declared. 'And it's about Douglas. He's been telling you that I'm dead set against him. Isn't that it?'

'That doesn't matter. Not between you and me,' she said.

'Wait a minute,' said Kildare. He went over to her, slowly.

'I see,' she said. 'I'm about to be examined, so I ought to face the light.'

She faced it, smiling.

He said, looking closely into her eyes: 'Douglas has been a big fellow in your life. He's the one you've formed a habit about. A habit of looking up to him.'

'That's right,' she agreed. 'And so?'

'Stop smiling that way.'

'All right. I'll give up smiling, Jimmy.'

He laughed. 'I mean, you're being so damned motherly and making a small boy out of me.'

'You're not small at all,' she said. 'You're a great big grown-up man, aren't you. Or aren't you?'

'Go on and laugh at me, then,' he said.

'I'm not laughing at all. I'm not even smiling, you see. Smiling isn't permitted.'

'I wonder why I am so batty about you?' said Kildare. 'Or am I?'

'Not very. Not very batty,' she said, shaking her head, and then facing the light again.

Kildare sighed. 'You're a cure, all right. Against taking myself seriously you're a fine cure, old girl. Look here. I want to be serious about something else.'

'Yes, doctor,' she said.

'About Douglas, and all that.'

'Yes, doctor,' she said.

'He thinks I'm a bit jealous of him, because I know what a big factor he is in your eyes; he thinks I'm opposing him because of some sort of reason like that. I'll tell you what I did. After I'd given him the introduction to Messenger, I rang Messenger and told him that I was afraid that Douglas wasn't altogether well, and then—'

She broke in quietly. 'That's all between you and Douglas—'

He interrupted in his turn: 'You're different from everybody else. I'll never make you out.'

'I hope not,' she said. 'That's what I'm afraid of.'

'You can smile, when you say that.'

'Thank you, doctor,' she said, smiling.

'I mean, ' said Kildare, 'you're going to keep us in two separate compartments of your mind. In this pigeonhole, Douglas. In the other pigeonhole, away over there, Jimmy.'

'It's a good way, don't you think?'

'Yes, I do.'

'So I don't need to face the light any more?'

'The fact is that you know I want to be helpful to Douglas.'

'But?'

'But I think he's not very well.'

'High blood pressure, or something like that?' she asked, carelessly.

'Ah,' said Kildare, 'you're worried, after all.'

'Oh, no.'

'You're worried,' he insisted. 'That's what I felt when you first came into the room. You think there may be something seriously wrong with him?'

'Isn't there?' she asked.

She put out both her hands in a quick gesture, as she asked the question, as if to prevent the wrong reply, and she kept smiling to invite the happy answer.

He took a note of these things for a moment. 'You've been frightened to death,' he announced.

'Not really.'

'Yes, frightened almost to death. Why didn't you come to me and ask questions, frankly?'

'I was afraid that you wouldn't be frank in the answers.'

'Not frank? With you?'

'Not about Douglas. You wouldn't be frank to me about Douglas.'

'Of course I would.'

'Don't lie even a little, Jimmy,' she said. 'I know you pretty well. You wouldn't tell me a word of the truth about Douglas if you thought it were something very serious. What do you think is wrong with him?'

'I don't know.'

'You hardly ever know—at first. You're like a hunting dog, and when the first scent of game comes down the wind you're not sure what it may be—a partridge, a grouse, a quail, even. So you have to study for a minute, and wrinkle your forehead, and half-close your eyes, and look inside and out. If I were a patient of yours, I'd be frightened when I saw that look come on your silly face, Jimmy, not what you know—but what do you begin to guess is wrong?'

'That he's burning himself up.'

'Overwork?'

'Yes. An obsession that keeps eating him, day and night.'

'Obsession,' she repeated, tasting the word and not liking it at all. 'Go on.'

'A fellow like Douglas can live on his nerve strength. Nerves are queer things.'

'Nerves,' she repeated, as she had done before, but this time with a slight shudder.

He was thinking about Douglas, not about the girl. He was re-seeing the case.

'He's let down, suddenly, by complete fatigue,' said the diagnostician, 'and then he rallies himself on the strength of his nerves. He forces himself ahead. Nerves are like shock troops. They can't be used all the time, though. And he's using them day and night.'

'That doesn't seem horribly serious, does it? To you?' she asked.

'We won't let it be serious,' said Kildare, bringing his attention back to her.

'Jimmy, Jimmy,' she sighed, 'you make me feel horribly better!'

CHAPTER SEVEN

... AND NO JIMMY

She kept on feeling better, that night and the next day—though in the mid-morning there was a telephone call from Douglas that troubled her just a little.

'Messenger is going to have his experts together this evening, and I'm to see them,' he said. 'What a fellow that Messenger is! Do you know one who will be there? P. J. Willoughby is one of them. You know what a devil *he* is?'

'Of course,' said she, though she'd never heard a word about the man.

'Then there's to be Samuel Chrisman. You know—the Harvard man.'

'Oh, yes,' said Mary, with equal ignorance.

'And Professor Walter O. Nissen.'

'Nissen!' she exclaimed, glad to recognize one of the names. 'But he's terribly famous and important, isn't he?'

'Nissen doesn't bother me. He's had plenty of space in the public prints, but that fellow Willoughby is the boy I'm going to watch and talk to. I'm going to aim at him. If I can hit him, the rest are easy.'

'You'll have them all on fire. How are you,

dear?' she asked.

'A little low, just now. Cold in the head, or something like that. Just the morning lowness, so that the notes I'm making don't seem to run along very well. They tangle up and bog down as if I were back in my freshman year in high school. But they'll straighten out later on.'

'Of course they will,' said Mary. 'I'm off duty at five. May I come over then to your room?'

'I'll be glad to have you. I might rehearse the speech a bit.'

'I hope it won't have to be a speech. Won't they simply ask questions?'

His response came quickly with a note of truculence.

'Why *shouldn't* it be a speech?'

'Because that's so exhausting, Douglas. And you ought to save your strength just a little, don't you think?'

'Look here. You've been talking to Jimmy about me.'

'Oh, no, Douglas. It's just that he thinks you live on your nerves a trifle too much.'

'Now listen to me, my lamb. Jimmy's a good lad, I'm sure. And some day he'll be a fine doctor, according to reports. But just now he's a little young—just a trifle young, eh?'

'Of course he is. And I'm not worried. I don't want you to think that I'm worried, dear. Neither is Jimmy. It's just that he thinks you overdo a trifle, and—'

'Just let that young man keep to his pills and pill boxes in his own world and not bother about me. These confounded little—well, let's not talk about him. I'll see you after five.'

'And take care of the cold, dear. You know, there's nothing better than salt and hot water and bicarbonate of soda snuffed up the nose.'

'Oh, I know all about that,' he chuckled, and rang off.

That was the only important event in her day until the afternoon mail brought her a letter in answer to the one she had written to her cousin. It was brief.

*   *   *

It *is* queer how names pop back into one's mind. But then it isn't surprising that you should think about our poor uncle! Haven't you ever heard his story? I don't know the details, and I'm sure I don't want to. I can look it up if you're really interested in such a black spot in the family record.

When I was a youngster, I remember hearing about his death in that institution. I remember the shudder that went through the family circle. They all stared at one another. I remember how sick and white my mother

66

looked and father ducked his head down and bit his lip, as if he'd been hit in the wind.

I don't think I ever heard them mention his name, after that. When I tried asking questions, they turned the subject. That made me more curious, and I tried to break them down but I didn't have any luck.

It was years later before I heard the story—briefly. It was too horrible for me to want to think of it afterwards. But I can look it up, I suppose. I can even find the date when he first began to go wrong.

But after all, *do* you really want to know? Hadn't family skeletons of such dimensions best be kept locked up in a dark closet and never shown to the light of day? Outside of him, I think our record is fairly clean.

*   *   *

She picked out the most pungent phrases and pieced them together. *I don't know the details and I'm sure you don't want to ... A black spot in the family record ... His death in that institution ... Too horrible for me to want to think of it ... The date when he first began to go wrong ... Family skeletons of such dimensions.*

Of it all, one word jumped off the page and remained in her mind: *Institution.*

There was only one kind of institution that she could think of, just then. And she remembered a day, long, long ago, when she had visited an institution for the 'restraint and cure' of the mentally unsound.

She got to her room and lay flat on the bed. She could not lie still. The words kept pounding at her. One drop of such a poison is enough to stain the record of a whole family, she felt. So, on the point of a pin, a billion fatal germs may be dropped into a city reservoir and there multiply until a whole community becomes diseased.

She got up and sat by the window. The air blew cold on her face but it brought also the mindless uproar of the city which came to her with such a voice that she pulled the window down. The silence inside the room was almost worse than the unhuman noise of the city. She remembered how she had sat there in horror after the first suspicion came into her mind.

'Something pathological about the case,' Jimmy had said to Messenger.

Pathological—pathological—pathological; she could remember, now, the first time the word had been seen on a page, to be looked up in the dictionary. Diseased.

And then, only moments ago, Jimmy had been saying: 'Obsession,' and afterward he had added: 'Nerves...'

*   *   *

That was what he feared about Douglas, of

course. A disease of the nerves, that polite word which doctors used when they mean the mind itself.

Had not she herself said over the telephone about a psychopathic case: 'Mr. Millan is a little nervous this morning. No, I'm so sorry that the doctor doesn't think it wise that he should be disturbed ... Oh, yes. Otherwise he's doing very well. Just as well as could be expected. Please ring again tomorrow.'

Poor Mr. Millan, then lying under a restraining sheet, with a straitjacket in the immediate offing as his poor brain crumbled and withered and disintegrated forever!

She wanted to rush at Kildare at once and ask the quick, dreadful question. But she knew she would get no answer. She knew how he would look down, in the quick way he had when he was withdrawing from a conversation. When he looked up again he would have a smooth, easy answer on the tip of his tongue.

They couldn't break through the defenses of Jimmy Kildare. Not even the great Gillespie had the ability to build up a higher wall of bland assurance: not even Gillespie knew so well how to allay fears. Her frightened eyes might as well probe and struggle with a great blank stone as to try to get at his hidden meanings.

He was almost an enemy; she almost hated

that calm manner, and that quiet voice which she had heard as he leaned over death-beds, giving even at the very last gasp a certain strange confidence that all would be well, all must be well, although the darkness at that moment was clouding the eyes.

She could get nothing of the truth from Kildare, nothing of the truth that he as yet only suspected. Only a suspicion, but how often was he wrong? How often does the hound truly blooded to foxes turn off on the rabbit's trail?

Should she go to him at once with her discovery that the blood of the Lamonts was in fact tainted? That might help him toward the dreadful truth.

Obsession—nerves; and in the background a Lamont who had died in an 'institution'!

She pressed her hands hard across her breast; and it was as if a child were being dragged from her by force. Her arms and her body and her soul were at the moment being emptied of the hope of having children. A starved virginity lay before her; and there would be no Jimmy, no Jimmy Kildare.

The agony was so great that flesh and spirit could not endure it for long. By a natural revulsion, hope possessed her, suddenly. The truth was that Jimmy was not sure; his suspicions did not even take a very definite line. And, even if they did, he was not always, not invariably right.

He could be wrong; he himself would be willing to admit that.

So it might come out right in the end.

It was possible for her to breathe again, little by little. Then there was the routine of work to return to. By the time she had taken a dozen steps she was a little ashamed of the passion of fear through which she had just passed. And hope, like a swarm of bees, multiplied rapidly.

CHAPTER EIGHT

BRING ANOTHER BRAIN

He lived in one of those hotels which make no pretense to grace or pleasantness. It was simply a concrete box cut across with concrete floors and with windows spotted in regular rows. It gave cheap housing; it had running water and cramped little bathrooms for every client; and it contributed a deathless blight to the spirit. But of course that was the sort of a place Douglas Lamont was sure to choose.

She found him walking up and down his floor with his hands clasped behind his back, his hair tousled, his shirt open at the scrawny throat. His coat had been thrown at a chair and slipped to the floor. Instead of a trim

71

belt, he wore braces that accentuated the hollowness of his chest.

There was a tangle of papers on the table; and she was surprised to see a bottle of bourbon, a siphon, and a tall glass with a bit of muddy amber liquid in the bottom of it. He never had been a drinker, far less a solitary one. To balance the whisky, there was a pot of coffee at the other end of the table, and a cup half filled.

None of these things really mattered to her. The first place she looked was into his eyes, in dread to see there that flickering and uneasy light which she had thought was inspiration, but which now, perhaps, might prove to be mere frenzy.

That burning eagerness was no longer in his eyes. Instead, there was a dull and rather blood-shot look. She welcomed that unpleasant change with a great sigh of relief.

'You're all right, Douglas,' she said. 'You're quite all right, aren't you?'

'All right?' he answered, gloomily. 'No, I'm a thousand miles from all right. My head's stuffed up by this infernal cold, or whatever it may be ... There's my speech, and it's no good. I can't get the words down. And in a couple of hours I've got to be standing in front of Willoughby, that devil Willoughby, with his baby face and his over-size brain.'

She was so relieved that she could not help

laughing a little.

'What does Willoughby matter? What does any of it matter?' she asked. 'You'll be all right when the time comes. You'll see.'

'Will I? Well, perhaps so. But don't stand there laughing. It's the test, for me. Mary, it's the great test and opportunity of my life.'

'Of course it is, and you'll go sailing through it. It's all the better not to be so—so nervous, Douglas.'

'You think so, but you don't know. I'll tell you the truth. I'm two men in one, it seems to me.'

She felt the shock of chilly terror again.

'What do you mean by that?' she asked, with the whole dreadful panorama of schizophrenia spreading out before her.

'I mean,' said Douglas Lamont, 'that some days I'm on edge. Everything seems easy, then. And other days, I'm rather down, rather sunk. Though I've never been as low as this before.'

She was laughing again, foolishly. She could have sung; she could have danced. She wished that Kildare could be with her in this room, now, to see what actually was the truth about Douglas. And yet Kildare himself had suggested it. She used his idea now.

'It's because you're been living on your nerves too much, of course,' she said. 'Why, Douglas, everyone has ups and downs. But

73

when you have a good day, you burn yourself up, and then there has to be a reaction. Don't you see? Don't you understand, dear?'

'I've never been this way before,' he said. 'Not even with a cold in the head and a fever and all that.'

'Are you sure you haven't a fever now?' she asked.

'I don't know. I don't think so.'

She put her hand against his cheek. It was, in fact, moist and cold. The temperature decidedly was subnormal. She dropped her fingers to his pulse. It was slow, very slow and dragging, with an occasional rapid pulsation that might be due to the alcohol.

'How much of that stuff have you been drinking?' she asked.

'I don't know. The rest of the bottle.'

'This afternoon?' she exclaimed.

For a third of the bottle was gone.

'No. I had a drink or two last night. Then this morning another when things started going badly.'

'Why, Douglas, that's all there is to it. It's just a little more than you're used to, and that's what's slowed you up. Jimmy says the stuff isn't good for anything—except to make a jolly time and break the ice.'

'Jimmy's wrong—perhaps not for the first time,' drawled Douglas. 'I've never worked so well in my life as I have since I started taking a drink or two before I went to bed at

74

night.'

'Really?'

'Yes, really.'

'But you hardly touched it, in the old days.'

'In the old days I was a sort of dead fish, wasn't I?'

'Not dead at all. But more easy-going.'

'I had a chill, one night when I went to bed, and I took a swig to warm me up. As a matter of fact, I slept like a log for five hours and woke up feeling like a new man. A sort of rebirth, if you know what I mean. I couldn't stay in bed. I had to hop up and get to work. There were ideas jumping through my brain so fast that I grabbed a pencil and paper and wrote out a sketch of them. Do you know what they were about?'

'What were they?' she asked, smiling, for this sight of him as a depressed, half-beaten poor devil was more and more of a relief to her. That fire—that crazy fire—was not in him now. As for that relative who died in the 'institution'—why, a single case like that makes no difference. There's bound to be one in every old family, is there not?

'What were the notes about, Douglas?'

'They were the first sketch of the project!'

'Really—in your mind while you were asleep?'

'Oh, I'd been thinking up that street for a good many years, of course. Every economist

75

does. Every economist dreams about solving the great question and apportioning a new sort of life and happiness to the underdogs. And that's the way solutions come, you see. You ponder over the problem for a long time. Then suddenly the truth shines in your eyes—the true way out.'

He sloshed some whisky into the glass, fed it a squirt from the siphon, and took a swallow. Then he shook his head.

'It doesn't seem to do any good,' he said.

'Give me the bottle, Douglas. Don't touch it again.'

'I tell you, it *can* help me, Mary. I hate the taste of the rotten stuff, but I never drink enough of it to get befogged. It's only that it gives me an up.'

'Take a hot bath and then lie down,' she commanded.

'Lie down? When I've got this stuff to work out?'

'Yes. A bath to relax you. And then lie down. In an hour, you'll be yourself again. And don't touch the whisky again.'

'Perhaps,' said he.

But now he sank down in the chair at the table and rested his chin on his fist. He seemed to her woefully small. Once more there came over her a swift pity for those men who work at the problems of the world, unregarded and forgotten, giving out life and blood as if it were bread.

'If you have an idea,' she said, 'go ahead and take notes on it. I'll sit here. I don't bother you, Douglas, do I?'

'No. I've got to get something down.'

He picked up a pencil, scowled at the distance as he poised his hand over the manila tablet, and prepared to write. A word or two went down on the paper. Again he lifted his head and stared into nothingness.

From where she sat, angling toward the window in the straight, uncomfortable chair, she could see him in three-quarters profile. And what she noted still was the dullness of the eye. No matter how he frowned with effort, the flash did not come back to him.

He was worked out, of course. She remembered feeling and looking like that when she had been up night after night studying for examinations. The time comes, of course, when there is not a single response to the will. The body fails; the will alone remains fixed and firm. So it was with her brother.

He shook his head and set his teeth. More words went down on the paper. And again there was the pause.

She got up and stood behind his chair, saying softly: 'There's only an hour and a half for you to get ready. Do as I say, my dear. Lie down. Close your eyes. I'll read you to sleep the way I used to a long time ago. You remember?'

'Sleep?' said his dull voice. 'I'm asleep now! There's no brain that will work for me.'

'Because you're tired out, Douglas. And you've *got* to be a little fresher for that interview. You really must do what I say. You know, I've learned a bit about how to take care of people.'

'It's Willoughby,' he muttered. 'If I could get by Willoughby, I'd be all right. If it weren't for that baby face, and the brain I know that goes behind it...'

Even then, in the tension, he had to yawn suddenly. And the sound was music to her. If ever there were normality, it was what she was seeing before her.

And yet it was a day of immense importance to him, she was perfectly aware. If he failed now, he might never be the same man again. That was one of the great Gillespie's ideas—that men may become punch-drunk in the ordinary struggles of life, just as pugilists become punch-drunk in the ring after many beatings. A man who had failed once too often may never find in himself, in the future, the sufficient fire and focal point. He remains inept, helpless, living on hope and not on accomplishment.

So a new sort of fear came to her; but compared with the horror that had been in her, by fits and starts for two whole days, this fear was nothing. It did not poison her own future, for one thing.

'I'm going out,' she said.

'No. Don't go. I'd rather have you here,' he said.

Still with his gaze fixed on the blankness of the wall, he made a gesture toward her, and she loved him for even that small appeal.

'I have to get something, and then I'll come right back,' she said.

'Don't bother getting things for me,' he said, as she went out the door. 'I don't need things; I need another brain.'

His voice was quite toneless; it was without life.

She closed the door and went hastily to the elevator. When she reached the street she went into a booth in a drugstore and telephoned to Kildare at the hospital.

CHAPTER NINE

MIST IN THE NIGHT

The quiet voice of Kildare presently was saying: 'I'm too busy to leave the hospital. Unless it's terribly important.'

'It's terribly important,' she answered. 'Douglas is really bogged down. The poor fellow is worn out, just as you said he was likely to be. You're so right about him, Jimmy. He's burning himself up. And now

79

that the nerve energy is gone, there's nothing to sustain him.

'In an hour and a half, he'll have to appear before Messenger and the experts, particularly a clever brain named Willoughby. Somehow he can't get himself started. The mind won't work.'

'Won't work?' repeated Kildare, quickly.

'That's it. You know how it is when you're dead fagged? You can't think.'

'Yes. I suppose so,' said Kildare.

'If you could come over and give him some sort of sedative, or whatever it is that he needs. If he simply can stop worrying, I'm sure that he'll pull himself together. He *has* to be right when he faces those four men.'

'I'll be there in a moment,' answered Kildare, and hung up.

He was with them, in fact, five minutes after she had returned to Douglas, to find him once more pacing the floor.

'I've asked Jimmy to come over,' she said.

She expected a violent reaction; but Douglas simply shook his head. 'Even if Jimmy were a *bad* doctor,' he said, 'I'd be glad to see him. Something ought to be done.'

When Kildare came in, he shook him quite warmly by the hand.

'It's kind of you to come over, like this,' he said. 'I've been excited and rude, talking to you before, Jimmy. You know, it seems to me that it wasn't I, but another man. It seems to me,' he added, 'that I must have been crazy to think that any idea of mine was so important that the whole world ought to know about it.'

Kildare, watching him, said: 'That's all right. There's nothing hurt, nothing broken at all. I'm sorry that you're upset.'

'It's Willoughby,' said Douglas. 'There's an economist with a brain as sure as a tiger's spring. If I slip—if I wave my arms and get too enthusiastic—that fellow will be the death of my project. And I don't seem to be able to pull myself together.'

He slumped into a chair and leaned back against the wall, shaking his head, his eyes half closed. Other words, half-born and unuttered, trembled on his lips. And in the corner of his mouth, as if he had gnawed his lip to the blood, there was a little fleck of red-stained saliva.

The reddened eyes, the loosened face-muscles, and above all that stain of red in the corner of the mouth began to have clear meaning to Kildare. His mind picked up the first surmise that had come to him when he first saw Douglas. It began to rush forward toward a conclusion.

He saw Mary, from the side, watching him with a confident smile.

'It's just exhaustion, isn't it, Jimmy?'

'Yes. Exhaustion. Of course,' said Kildare.

'Then don't be so grim about it.'

He passed a hand up across his face and back over his head.

Sometimes the whole profession of medicine was abhorrent to him. Sometimes it seemed to Kildare that—body, mind and spirit—man is a hopeless case of decadence and of real decay with no soundness at the core. He felt these things now, and more sharply than he ever had felt them before, as he stared at Mary's brother with a growing conviction.

The girl was saying, cheerfully: 'You know, Douglas has been slipping into some bad habits. He never had this nervousness until a few years ago. Then he started having a drink or two before he went to bed. And he began to wake up with his head full of new ideas—like the project, for instance.'

'Ah! He woke up with a head full of new ideas?' repeated Kildare.

'That's all right, isn't it?'

'Of course it's all right,' said Kildare. 'I'll be back in a minute.'

When he had gone out, she said to Douglas: 'It's all right. He knows what's wrong.'

'Does he?' asked Lamont, dully. 'He doesn't talk a great deal, does he?'

'Not when he sees the truth about a case. He doesn't talk. He just does something about it. He'll be back and fix you up so that you'll be a new man. You'll drive through Willoughby like a dream.'

Kildare came back and started to prepare to give an injection. Lamont obediently rolled up his sleeve.

'I like to know why things like this are done,' he said. 'You'd better tell me, Jimmy. Just what do you think is wrong with me? I might have an attack of these blue devils some other time when you're not around.'

'It's nervous exhaustion,' said Kildare. 'It comes from making efforts that are a little too big for your skin to hold. You see?'

'I see,' said Lamont, yawning.

Mary, glancing from one to the other, kept her eyes still on Kildare, even when the needle went into the scrawny arm of her brother. For she knew that Kildare was lying.

She could not have attributed her knowledge to anything other than a special instinct or perception which she sometimes possessed when she was with him—or was there not a slight arching of the brows, a slight brightening of the eyes, as if he were making a slight, a very slight extra effort in the direction of extreme candor?

Perhaps he overdid the frankness a little bit. It is a fault, she knew, which grows on doctors. The bedside manner may become a sort of conversational poison.

The injection completed, Douglas was rolling down his sleeve again.

He was relaxed now.

'Now you lie down, close your eyes, and relax,' said Kildare.

Douglas obeyed. He threw his arms out wide as if sleep were an embrace he waited for.

'You'll feel a bit of warmth,' said Kildare. 'Then sleepiness. Don't fight against it.'

'As long as I'm right for the Messenger party,' said Douglas, yawning. 'That's all that matters.'

He sighed deeply.

'Don't think forward to anything. Just try to relax,' said Kildare.

He picked up Douglas' coat and pulled it over the middle of his body. Then he sat down and took the pulse. Counting it, he looked up with the unseeing eyes of thought that dwelt vaguely on Mary and then shifted away.

She was a little troubled by that shifting away from her, as if she might be able to probe into a secret. Some of her sense of security began to leave her; and yet there remained a great warmth about her heart as she saw the two of them side by side.

Kildare rose from the bedside, presently, as the breathing of Douglas became regular, deep.

He went to the telephone and asked, quietly, for a number. Douglas did not stir. He was soundly asleep.

'He'll be awake in time for the meeting?' asked Mary.

Kildare stared back at her with the same empty, thoughtful eyes.

Presently he was saying: 'This is Kildare. May I speak to Mr. Messenger?'

He paused. Mary Lamont stood up and went hurriedly to him. She stood behind his chair, full of question, but too much the trained nurse to interrupt.

After a moment Kildare was saying: 'Hello, Mr. Messenger. I'm sorry to tell you that Douglas Lamont is all out of sorts tonight. A cold coming on. And he's been overworking. The fact is that I've put him to bed...

'Yes, I know about the meeting, but I felt that it was more important to make sure of his health. Can you possibly postpone it to another time? ... That's kind of you. Yes, he *is* impressive. But tonight he wouldn't be able to do himself justice ... Of course I will. Goodbye.'

He hung up the telephone.

'Jimmy!' whispered Mary Lamont. 'You haven't knocked him out, have you? He'll be almost insane if he wakes up and finds out that he wasn't at the meeting.'

Kildare shrugged his shoulders. He took out a card and scribbled a prescription on the back of it.

'You can step out and have this

prescription filled,' said Kildare. 'He'll sleep quietly until you're back.'

'Yes,' she said, with the old fear coming back in her a little. 'Jimmy, what is it?'

'Why, you can see for yourself,' he said. 'He's exhausted. He couldn't make good sense. He couldn't drive his point home, if he went to see Messenger and those experts tonight. Messenger will call another meeting—perhaps for tomorrow night.'

'Then there's nothing lost?' she asked.

'Why, of course not. But a great deal gained, I hope.'

'It isn't something *more* than exhaustion?' she insisted.

'Why? What makes you think it might be?'

'Because you've grown horribly distant, all at once. There's a thousand miles between us, Jimmy.'

'We'll go out together,' said Kildare. 'You're a little dizzy with concern, because it's Douglas. Try to think that it's simply anybody—a casual case in the hospital. That's what you'll have to do.'

She kept silent on the way down in the elevator. They came out onto the sidewalk and found a thin mist of rain falling that brightened the sidewalks to silver under the street lamps, to glowing orange near the neon signs.

Kildare, in the open, paused and lifted his head as if he were looking up to a clean, starry sky, filling his lungs with pure air. She took note of that, also. He had been through some sort of an ordeal.

Then he said, in his most casual manner: 'You'd better stay with him through the night. I suppose you can sleep in the big chair, Mary? I'd stay, but I have to push through the report for Gillespie.'

'Of course I'll stay,' she answered. 'It's as serious as that?'

'I don't want him to be alone when he wakes up. You know—he'll see what the time is and realize that he's missed the Messenger meeting. That would be a horrible shock, wouldn't it?'

'Of course.'

'I think he'll sleep through the night. Just get that prescription filled and when he *does* begin to wake up, telephone to me. I'll come right over. I want to see what the reactions are after he's slept.'

'How long before he wakes up?'

'I think he'll carry through the night, but I'm not sure.'

'And—Jimmy, it's all right?'

'Of course it's all right,' said Kildare, and then turned away from her and walked off, always hurrying, always vainly trying to overtake the crowd of duties that lay ahead.

She watched him out of sight around the corner; and a voice inside her kept saying, *But he's lying. It isn't all right.*

CHAPTER TEN

AN EYE AND A GIFT

Kildare walked all the way back to the hospital but he could not walk the preconception out of his mind. The whir and slosh of wheels on the wet streets ate into his mind like the noise of buzz-saws. It was not Douglas Lamont that held his attention, but Mary, Mary, Mary, like a sad song.

The walk was not long enough to get the ache out of his heart. He turned toward Mike Ryan's saloon. Twenty steps from it he heard a noise of heavy scuffling, so he went in at the family entrance and found Joe Weyman engaged with his famous big fists on a fellow still bigger than the ambulance driver.

They fought with gasping, silent ferocity, and even stepped softly, in and out, for fear the noise of their trampling might bring in the police; and there was a rich delight of battle in the eyes of both.

A dozen spectators stood around the room, with Mike Ryan in person presiding over the shennanigan. No one spoke above a murmur. There was hardly a sound louder than the heavy smacking of fists against head and body that went home, now and then, like the clapping of hands.

Mike Ryan's heart was equally divided, it seemed. When he saw Kildare, he side-stepped toward him like a crab, and seized his arm.

'What will you have, doc?' he asked. And then he whispered: 'Go it, Danny—go it, Joe.'

He encouraged the fighters as a cheer-leader encourages the rooting section, waving his arms frantically. Danny, a big, black-haired Irishman, fought with a sneering contempt, as if confident that youth and twenty extra pounds were sure to win for him; Weyman was the rushing aggressor. A moment later, Danny hit him away with a fine one-two and cornered him.

'The wind, Joe,' said Kildare. 'Come in on the wind!'

Through a smear of blood, Weyman glanced across at Kildare. His grin of acknowledgment bared his teeth. Then he brought up a lifting punch that doubled Danny like a jack-knife, his guard low. It was simple as drinking beer for Weyman to whip the next blow to the chin; and Danny sat down heavily.

He started to rise, still embracing his aching stomach, but Ryan stepped before him.

'That's enough, Danny,' he said. 'You're clean gone, poor lad. It's over, Danny. It was a good go. You done fine and we're proud to know you.'

Danny slumped into a chair. He gasped: 'I could of beat him black and blue, but I couldn't handle his damned big fists and the brains of the doc. Not all at the same time.'

'Of course you couldn't,' said Ryan.

Kildare was opening his medical kit and getting out tape and iodine and small surgical pads.

'Sit down here beside Danny,' he said to Weyman.

The ambulance driver obediently took the chair next to the Irishman.

'I thought you had me with the one-two,' said Joe. 'It's a honey, that one. Where'd you get it?'

'I seen Gene Tunney in the slow movies,' said Danny. 'And I'm gunna have another go at you as soon as I can see good again, Joe.'

'Sure,' said Weyman. 'That's the way to talk, Danny. If it wasn't for you, I wouldn't have no taste for me beer tonight.'

Kildare swabbed off their faces. They submitted with cherubic patience, like two children, their heads tilted back.

'Wow!' said Danny. 'You're burning me alive, doc!'

'Be still,' said Kildare, and put a small pad and tape over an inch-long cut under Danny's eye. He took a glass of beer from the hand of Mike Ryan and had a good swallow from it. 'You're fat, Danny, and soft in the belly.'

'I am that,' agreed Danny. 'But you shouldn't of taken sides with Joe. The big squarehead could of beat me on the jaw all night and never made me feel it. You shouldn't play favorites, doc. It ain't like you.'

'No, it ain't like the doc,' agreed several voices.

'I was afraid that you'd murder him, Danny,' said Kildare. 'I saw he was all at sea with his eyes blinking and his brains gone completely. And I wouldn't have you up Salt Creek because of a worthless fellow like Joe ... Have you shaken hands?'

They grinned at one another and shook hands.

'And when you want another fight, Danny,' said Kildare, 'don't pick on the old men like Joe Weyman.'

'Old? Me?' said Joe. 'I could lick two like him every night of the week, and three on Sunday before breakfast.'

'Be still,' said Kildare. 'Your wind's gone, your timing's out, and your feet are bogged down in mud. You're only half a man, Joe.'

Weyman raised sad eyes to Kildare, found a frown on his face, and drew a long sigh.

'You're a fine picture of a man,' said Kildare, when he had finished. 'Look at yourself! And what will you say when they see you at the hospital tomorrow?'

'He fell down stairs by forgetting where his feet were going,' suggested Mike Ryan.

'Somebody closed a door in his face,' said another sympathizer.

Kildare finished his beer, and turned to the door. A chorus entreated him to stay. He shook his head and went on. On the sidewalk, Joe Weyman came lumbering after him.

'Are you mad at me, doc?' he said. 'I mean not for the fighting, but because God knows it's my nature and you can't go against God, can you? But for letting a young fathead like Danny lay a finger on me? Are you mad and disgusted at me, doc?'

'It's the booze, Joe,' said Kildare. 'He never would have been able to touch you, but you've whittled yourself away with the liquor until all the spring has gone out of you. You can't hit straight when you can't see straight.'

'I'll give it up,' said Weyman. 'I'll go back and have just one goodnight drink, and then I'm home.'

'You're home without the drink,' said Kildare.

Joe Weyman stopped stock still.

'Ah, you're sour at me, doc,' he said, sadly.

'I am,' agreed Kildare. 'Go over to the hospital and resign from the ambulance today. Do what I tell you, or you're going to take a ride pretty soon that will land you in the morgue.'

He went on like that, without another word, and entered the hospital past the switchboard presided over by Sally, the telephone operator. He paused and leaned on the desk.

'Good evening, doctor,' she was saying. 'He's asleep. He's been asleep for more than half an hour. I hope he gets in another good hour, poor man, before he's wakened.'

He knew she spoke of Gillespie. The whole hospital seemed to be conscious of the few intervals when pain and his will to work permitted the old man to relax in sleep.

'Sally,' said Kildare, 'what about you and Joe?'

'You mean Weyman?' said Sally. 'You mean that four-footed bear of an ambulance driver?'

'I mean my good old friend, Joe Weyman,' said Kildare.

She grew sober, by degrees, staring at him in a little apprehension.

'Marry him, Sally, will you?' said Kildare.

'Him? Marry *him*?' she echoed.

'You like him, don't you?'

'I don't mind wasting a minute with him, now and then. But who'd take a fellow like that serious?'

'Marry him, Sally,' said Kildare. 'He's too

young for his years. He's going down hill.'

'I'm sure he can go where he pleases, as far as I'm concerned,' said Sally, shrugging her shoulders.

Kildare turned away from the desk.

'But—doc?' she called, standing up from the board.

He faced her again.

'How close to the bottom of the hill is the idiot?' she asked.

'Not so very close. There's still room for him to have a hard fall,' said Kildare.

'Booze?' asked Sally.

'Booze,' agreed Kildare.

'I'll have a talk with him,' said Sally, darkly.

'Do that,' he advised. 'Tell him you love him; and ask him to marry you.'

'*I* ask *him*?' cried Sally, enraged. 'What sort of a man is he if *I* have to ask him?'

'Sally,' said Kildare, 'why do you waste my time being proud?'

She stared at him. A great flush began to run up her thin face.

'I don't know, doc,' she whispered. 'I'm sorry.'

'Don't be sorry. Be happy,' said Kildare. 'Joe is the biggest heart in the whole world; and you're bright enough for two. Do you see how it fits?'

'Yes,' whispered Sally.

Kildare, leaving her still staring, passed on

down the hall. He went up to his room. Enough city light reflected from the misty sky to show him the gray, tumbled bed on which his roommate was sleeping. The dimness washed across the lower part of the room like dirty water, with chairs and shoes, and heaps of fallen clothes lying here and there.

He wanted sleep so badly that there was an ache behind his eyes; but he knew that if he lay down the faces of Mary and Douglas would look in on his mind and rouse him again.

Instead of getting into pyjamas, he put on his whites, finding them in the dark for fear of waking the sleeper. Then he went down to the accident room.

He passed Sally on the way and found her smiling and singing to herself as she sat back before the idle board, her hands in her lap. She blushed again when she saw Kildare.

'Is he still asleep?' asked Kildare.

'Yes—bless him,' said the girl.

'I'm in the accident room if he wakes up,' said Kildare.

'Accident room? You've got to have your fun, doc, don't you? I'll let you know. The first minute he stirs he always hollers for you.'

It was dull down in the accident room. A new staff physician was idling about, besides the usual pair of internes and Bixby, one of the residents like Kildare. A broken collarbone was being repaired; a woman with a crying jag was getting a sedative and good advice; and they were putting a cold, wet blanket around a middle-aged man with a shag of gray beard on his chin.

That was what caught the eye of Kildare. He stepped closer and watched the nurses at work.

'Heat stroke, doctor,' said one of them.

He glanced at the pale face of the sick man.

'Out of a boiler room,' said the second nurse. 'They're mankillers, some of those boiler rooms.'

'Get that blanket off him,' said Kildare. 'Get it off fast! And turn off the fan. It'll kill him quick. He needs stimulants.'

The staff physician was coming slowly across the room.

Kildare went on: 'And saline solution, intravenously. Give him an injection at once.'

'But Doctor Kimberley ...' began the first nurse.

'I'm Kimberley,' said the staff physician. 'You're one of the residents, young man, aren't you? I'm Kimberley, of the staff. And since when is it in order in this hospital for a young resident to reverse orders?'

'I beg your pardon, sir,' said Kildare. 'In the accident room—'

'The accident room is the accident room, I agree,' said Kimberley, 'but don't let accidents happen to your professional manners, my very young friend.'

'Sorry, sir,' broke in Kildare. 'This isn't a heat stroke, I'm afraid. It's heat exhaustion. Please get that blanket off him. It'll kill him, Doctor Kimberley.'

'A man out of a boiler room—Do you mean that you're changing my diagnosis right under my nose?'

'I'm talking about a man's life,' said Kildare.

'I'll have your name, my friend,' said Kimberley, icily.

'James Kildare, sir,'

Kimberley dropped his notebook back into his pocket.

'Gillespie's alter ego?' he said. 'Young Kildare? I've heard about you. Let me have a look at this fellow ... By Jove you're right. I should have noticed that pale face. Get the blanket off him ... Kildare, I've been a good deal of a fool; but thank God you've put me right.'

'Telephone for you, doctor,' said an attendant to Kildare.

'Sorry about everything,' said Kildare earnestly.

'Don't be sorry,' said Kimberley. 'Young genius is better than old brains any day.'

At the telephone Sally's voice was saying:

'He's awake, doc! And he's roaring. Better come on the run.'

'Thanks,' said Kildare, and hurried for the door.

He noticed, as he went out, that the nurses, the attendants, the internes, even Bixby, went about their work with their heads bent a little, exchanging sly smiles. And poor Kimberley, his head erect, his face very red, endured the ridicule like a man.

It hurt Kildare. And most of all he was struck by that word 'genius' which had been applied to him. It was not the first time that it had floated in the air near him, in the Blair General Hospital. And he hated the sound of it.

He felt small pride in his accomplishments. The eye which saw perhaps a little deeper than the eyes of other men was a gift to him from nature. And all the rest was another gift, from the old, dying hands of Gillespie. So he walked with his head bowed, like a burden bearer, as he hurried toward Gillespie's rooms.

CHAPTER ELEVEN

DOCTORS MEAN DEATH

The line which formed in Gillespie's waiting room and flowed all day long and most of the night through his office was handled twice as fast when Kildare assisted his chief directly. Sometimes he took them in Gillespie's office and passed them on to the great man behind him; but usually he examined them in his own office and sent them in to Gillespie's with a brief note of diagnosis and recommended treatment, which Gillespie checked.

Now, for several hours, they labored in this fashion until the line dwindled away to nothing. After that, Kildare dropped on his couch and closed his eyes. He had learned how to sleep at a moment's notice; but he could not sleep now. In a moment he was up again and back in Gillespie's office.

He found the great old man turning the pages of a thick medical tome, checking passages with a thick blue pencil that made huge swipes in the margin.

'So you missed again, eh?' he said, without looking up.

'Where, sir?' asked Kildare.

'He doesn't even know where!' snarled

Gillespie. 'He's beaten and doesn't even know that there was a battle! Can't you remember any place where you might have slipped?'

'Yes, sir.'

'What one, then?'

'The woman with the cardiac decomposition.'

'And what do you think might have been wrong?'

'Adenoma of the thyroid gland.'

'And so?'

'I asked for an X-ray.'

'But you missed something else. Jennings, young Doctor Kildare! You missed on Jennings!'

He stabbed a forefinger at Kildare and made a horrible face.

'Jennings?' said Kildare, frowning, trying to remember.

'Fibrillary contractions—did you notice those? And the deep reflexes increased?'

Kildare held out a hand as if he were about to grasp something out of thin air. He shut the hand hard, finally, as if he had made the catch.

'Amyotrophic lateral sclerosis!' he exclaimed.

'That's it. A little late, however; just a little late, young Doctor Kildare.'

'I told him to come back,' said Kildare, flushing. 'I wasn't satisfied and wanted another look at him. I wasn't sure.'

'But would he have come?'

'I don't know.'

'That's what you had to find out. Don't forget that people hate hospitals. We think of ourselves as little demigods sitting on perches for the world to applaud. But we're wrong.

'People hate us and our hospitals. We dispense medicine; also we dispense pain. The smell of carbolic acid is a horror that steals the hearts out of men and turns their blood to water. Because they connect it with hospital corridors, and death, Kildare, death!

'So make sure of your people. Jennings never would have come back. He would have stayed away and gone on wasting, wasting, without knowledge of what was wrong.'

Kildare took a long breath.

'It hurts, eh?' said Gillespie.

'A little,' admitted Kildare.

'Well, my fine friend, *I'll* not praise you,' said Gillespie. 'No man can be perfect, but perfection is the only thing you can try for, young Doctor Kildare. Work like a devil or an angel all day long, but when you go to bed at night, take some of your errors, some of your mistakes, and lie down with them in your heart.'

'It's true, sir,' said Kildare.

'Dream about your mistakes; dream that you are making more of them; and wake up in the morning determined that you'll spot every feature of a disease as fast as it shows its face ... Now what the devil is wrong with you?'

'Nothing, sir.'

'There *is* something wrong.'

'No, sir.'

'Damn it, Kildare, don't argue with me. Less than three months ago there was another case of amyotrophic lateral sclerosis, and you spotted it all by yourself. Less than three months ago! The Kildare I know isn't the fellow who forgets such things. The Kildare who works with me never forgets *anything*. You hear?'

'Yes, sir,' said Kildare.

'Because if you *do*,' said Gillespie, 'I'm damned if I want anything to do with you!'

'No, sir,' said Kildare.

'Now tell me about it, Jimmy.'

'About amyotrophic—'

'No, damn it! About yourself! Where's the pain? Heart or head or conscience?'

'There's really nothing wrong with me.'

'Of course not. Good pulse. Normal temperature. Battered around the eyes because you need sleep—that's all. Strange about you young dogs. You have to sleep. Horrible habit, sleep. You've got to cut down on it. Nine-tenths of sleep is damned, foolish self-indulgence. You hear?'

'Yes, sir.'

'But I'm not talking about your physical condition ... Jimmy, what's aching in your heart?'

Kildare said: 'I think I'd better get some of that sleep you were talking about. I'd better indulge myself a little.'

'You're going to be proud, are you?' demanded Gillespie.

'I'm going to sleep, sir, if you don't mind.'

'Changing the subject on me; being proud,' roared Gillespie, 'sticking your head in the air—pretending you have a right to a life and a mind of your own, are you? I'll put an end to that damned quickly! You think you ought to have a decent privacy for your own affairs, do you?'

'I hope I have that right, sir.'

'Start hoping something else,' shouted Gillespie. 'I never heard anything so damned silly in my life. Young man, everything that goes on in you, from the digestion of starch to the tickle in the palm of your ambitious damned young hand, from the way you feel when you see the sun rise to the tear in your eye when a worthless damned baby dies—none of those things are your private property. They're a communal affair. They belong first of all to *me*!'

Kildare stared at him.

'Surprised, are you?' asked Gillespie.

'No, sir,' said Kildare.

'If you were surprised, I'd be through with
103

you,' said Gillespie. 'If you'd known me these months and I still could surprise you, I'd turn you out. If you didn't know me better than that, I'd give up all hope of making you the greatest damned diagnostician that draws breath on this earth.

'So come out with it! What is this affair that you have the infernal effrontery to think is a private affair?'

Kildare smiled.

Then he said, slowly: 'There's Mary's brother, Douglas Lamont. He's a sick man.'

'Well? Well? What of it? You're not marrying the whole damned family, I hope, when you marry Mary?'

'The symptoms,' said Kildare, 'might interest you.'

'*All* symptoms interest me,' said Gillespie.

'When I first saw him, he was below par, rather sleepy in action and appearance, very relaxed. While he was talking to me, he seemed about to go to sleep. Actually, for a moment there *was* an instant of complete relaxation.'

'That's nothing,' said Gillespie. 'As a matter of fact it's fairly common for people with something on their minds to go to sleep for a second while they're talking. Was that the way it happened?'

'Yes, sir,' said Kildare. 'But there was something peculiar about this instance. A moment later, he was talking with tremendous vigor. He was on fire.'

'Ah?' said Gillespie.

'That energy lasted for some time. This evening I've seen him again. He was utterly relaxed again. He had an important meeting to attend and couldn't rally himself to put together the address he had to make. A man with his mind crowded with his own ideas, ordinarily; and yet they wouldn't come out and stand in line for him in the pinch.

'Accustomed, during the last few years, to taking a drink or two before he goes to bed. And then he often wakes up and finds himself on fire with new ideas. As if his brain had been working in his sleep.

'Well, his brain wasn't working last evening. He was soggy, like a drunkard on a morning after. I watched him closely. He was perfectly uncoordinated. He seemed to have bitten his lip or his tongue. There was a little red stain of blood and saliva in the corner of his mouth.'

'There was what?' snapped Gillespie.

'A stain of blood—'

'What is he to Mary?' asked Gillespie.

'Her brother, sir.'

'Yes, yes, yes! But what does that mean? A brother may be a distant relative that you wish the devil would take away from you, or a brother may be closer to you than all the friends in the world. Now, what is he to Mary?'

'He's a nervous, rather disagreeable fellow, at times,' said Kildare. 'His mind is so set on doing a great good for the world that he doesn't mind his manners all the time. But Mary knows him well. He was almost a father to her when she was a youngster. He's nearly everything to her.'

'I'm sorry,' said Gillespie, after a moment of thought.

Kildare had turned pale.

'You think what I think, sir?' he managed to ask.

'What do you prescribe?'

'A sedative.'

Gillespie leaned forward.

'Ah?'

'Phenobarbital. A large dose.'

'And then?'

'More phenobarbital, and a diet to start today.'

'Ah ha,' said Gillespie. 'Sedative and diet.'

'There's only one question, sir. Do you agree with me?'

'How can I agree with anything, when I haven't seen the patient?' roared Gillespie.

'I only mean—you think I may have been right?'

Gillespie reached out a quick paw and caught the hand of Kildare.

'It all may be a nasty mess, unless it's properly handled. Poor Mary! Jimmy, I'm afraid that for once you've been right.'

CHAPTER TWELVE

AS IF ... GOODBYE

In spite of all that lay on his mind, Kildare managed to sleep two or three hours before the telephone called him. Mary Lamont's excited, trembling voice came to him over the wire:

'I'm in terrible trouble, Jimmy. Douglas has woken up. He was in a fury when he discovered what had happened to him. It's a great treason, he seems to feel. I'm guilty, along with you. I must have known what you intended to do, and so I'm a party to the treachery. And everything is horrible.'

'Have you been crying? Are you crying now?'

'Not very much.'

'Ah, damn him!' said Kildare.

'Darling, he can't help himself. It's his great project that we've struck down, he thinks. He doesn't care about himself. He really doesn't. But he feels as if we'd betrayed the whole nation, in a sense—all the poor, unhappy people in the nation have been betrayed!'

'I understand,' said Kildare.

'And finally he asked me to leave the room. When he feels that he can see me again, he'll send for me. It's simply frightful, Jimmy. He's cold as iron, and reserved, and looks at me as if I were simply a *creature*.'

'I'll go see him.'

'No, no, no! Please, Jimmy. Don't go near him. That would be terrible. He'd say things to you that you'd never forget.'

'I've got to get to him. Have you had that prescription filled yet?'

'Not yet. I'll go now. I'll have it done.'

'At the corner drugstore?'

'Yes.'

'I'll pick it up when I arrive. You go on back to the Nurses' Home, Mary.'

'No, I'll stay here and wait for you.'

'Do what I tell you, Mary. Go home and sleep.'

'All right. I'll go, Jimmy.'

But when he reached the drugstore and picked up the prescription he found that she was waiting for him, nevertheless.

'I wanted to do what you told me,' she said. 'But somehow when I started thinking of you walking into the room of Douglas—I mean, it's so impossible that he'd accept a prescription from you now, you know.'

'I'll *make* him accept it.'

'You don't mean that you'd use force?'

'No, no. Of course not.'

They stood outside the store. The dawn was commencing to work through the mist of the night. It covered the pavements with

108

its greasy lights. Dirt of the night clotted the gutters. There still were street lamps shining like little captured moons ranged up and down.

'Jimmy, I want to beg you not to go to him.'

'There's no use begging. I'll have to go. Unless he'll accept another doctor.'

'He won't hear of a doctor from now on, as long as he lives.'

'That's why his mind has to be changed.'

'Jimmy, do you mean that his life is in danger?' she asked.

He watched the tremor of her lips.

'I mean that he has to take care of himself,' he said.

'You won't tell me anything, I suppose?'

'You're all apart,' he said. 'Take hold of yourself.'

'Yes,' she whispered. 'I'll take hold of myself. I'll be all right. But please tell me something.'

'Why should I tell you what you can see for yourself? Can't you see that he's soft, and life is a regular sandpaper for him? It's rubbing him out. There's hardly anything left of him. He ought to be wrapped in cotton batting for a while.'

'You mean that's all? He's sound, really?'

'You know, Mary,' he said, 'I never saw a clearer proof of the old rule: get nurses and doctors outside of your own family. You're all in jitters because of Douglas. If it had been a case in the hospital, you wouldn't be so on edge, would you?'

'No, Jimmy.'

'Then you run along to the Home and get some sleep.'

'While you go up to Douglas?'

'Probably.'

She shut her eyes tight.

'I hate that,' she said.

'There won't be any physical violence,' said Kildare.

'I don't know. He's really beside himself.'

'There won't be any fighting,' said Kildare calmly.

'Let me talk to you a minute more.'

'As long as you please.'

'It was phenobarbital last night, wasn't it?' she asked.

'Yes.'

'But ordinarily you don't go in for that quite so much—do you?'

'Perhaps not.'

'And then when I found out that the prescription is loaded with it—'

'Ah, a druggist who talks about his prescriptions?'

'I told him that I was the nurse on the case.'

She searched his clouded face.

'I mean, Jimmy, it was rather a long time, and there was nothing to do except talk, you know.'

'It was a bad idea, that's all,' said Kildare.

'You think that Douglas ought to be kept really low with the sedative—for quite a time?'

'The fellow's nerves have to rest, don't they?'

'Yes, Jimmy. Of course they do. I can't help it, if—'

'If what?'

'I don't know. I don't think I've taken a single deep breath for days.'

'Why not, old dear?'

'From the first minute you laid eyes on Douglas you thought that there was something seriously wrong with him.'

'Have you forgotten last evening? That was pretty serious, wasn't it? I'd like to prescribe three months on Florida beaches, you know.'

'Just that? Nothing else?'

'You're like the others, Mary. You forget that sleep and rest are the best medicines. All our truck—or most of it—is simply a substitute. Give his body a chance to take care of itself.'

'I suppose that's right. Only—there was so *much* of the phenobarbital. And really, Douglas is not very large—to absorb such doses, I mean.'

She came to the entrance of the hotel. Its brass name plate was grimy black.

'History is going to be made up there,' she said. She tried to smile. 'It doesn't matter to the rest of the world but it matters everything to me. It's more than nations falling. What happens between you and Douglas, I mean. Jimmy, try to make a way for me to come back to him, will you?'

'I'll do everything I can, of course.'

'Say one last thing to me.'

Kildare stared into her face and saw the terrible urgency there. At length he said slowly:

'As if this were goodbye, or something?'

'I almost feel that way about it.'

'Remember, you're not to be silly. You've got a set of nerves as wobbly as Douglas', almost.'

'It's in the family, perhaps?'

He frowned.

'What are you trying to make of this, anyway?'

'I don't know. Nothing.'

He went through the revolving door. When he turned, looking back, she still was standing there, looking after him, and the mist on the glass of the door obscured her as if a heavy rain were falling.

He waved. She waved in return, and he faced forward into the gloom of the hotel lobby, with the staleness of tobacco smoke rank in the air.

CHAPTER THIRTEEN

MEET DOCTOR HOUDINI

When he knocked at the door of Douglas Lamont's room a crisp, clear voice called: 'Yes? Come in.'

He pushed the door open. Lamont sat at his table, writing busily.

'Well?' he asked, looking steadily at Kildare.

'I've brought something that you need to take,' said Kildare, entering the room and closing the door.

'Kind of you,' said Lamont, 'but I don't need a doctor. I particularly don't need you.'

'Will you let me talk to you for a while?'

'You can see that I'm very busy, doctor,' said Lamont. He gestured to the papers on the table.

'I was at a halt last night. The sleep which you so kindly assured me last night probably has ruined my prospects forever. But at least it gave my mind a chance to clear up.'

'I was sorry about that,' said Kildare. 'It seemed necessary.'

'I believe,' said Lamont, 'that unsolicited services from a doctor—that is to say, when a doctor is asked to do one thing, and deliberately does another—What are the

113

ethics of your profession, doctor? Or do you bother about trivialities such as ethics?'

'I hoped we wouldn't have to talk like this,' said Kildare. 'Do we? Do we have to go through a lot of recriminations? I was doing what seemed absolutely the best thing for you.'

'I suppose it did,' said Lamont.

As if he could not endure the sight of Kildare for another moment, he rose and walked to the window. There he stood with his hands locked hard together behind his back. The tension that drew upon him kept him trembling a little.

Kildare laid his medical case on the end of the table and waited. He was trying to find words, but that narrow, rigid back drove words out of his mind.

'They're getting up now,' said Lamont, waving toward the gray of the outer morning. 'A lot of poor devils, out there, are getting up, dragging on their clothes, getting ready for the morning shift. They're people like me: narrow shoulders, and bent, and a little twisted, and scrawny necks, and knock-knees, and dragging feet.

'They haven't any hope to straighten them. They haven't a chance to breathe decent air. They haven't a chance because they haven't been taught to work; and the only way to teach them to use their hands is to give them a hunger, a desire to get at the soil, or to build, to make, to create.

'A fellow who has built even as much as a cowbarn is set aside from tens of millions who never have built anything. He has found happiness and he knows how he can find more ... You ever think of such things, doctor?'

'A good deal. More, since I've heard you talk about the problem; a great deal more since you've suggested a solution.'

Lamont whirled about and faced him.

'Why do you have to be mealy-mouthed?' he asked through his teeth. 'I know what you think!'

'Tell me what I think,' asked Kildare, curiously.

'You think that it's all an illusion. I tell you, Kildare, hell is paved with people like you who take it for granted that at first glance they understand everything and can weigh possibilities and probabilities.

'You say that the whole project is a fairy tale. But I tell you that nothing except the improbable is worth working for. Will you believe that, a little? It's improbable that men are better than beasts. It's improbable that right and justice are stronger than might and tyranny. It's all damned improbable.

'But by degrees the world works forward. It comes closer and closer to the light. Now and then a wave of darkness overtakes it, but only for a moment. The day will come when

115

every man will be born with a right, an acknowledged right, to freedom, to full life, and to happiness. There will be no villains then. There will only be an occasional fool.

'I beg your pardon for talking about things like this to you. I know you're laughing up your sleeve.'

'I'm not laughing, Douglas,' said Kildare.

'Ah, but you are. You and Mary will sit together and snicker over this, later in the day.'

'You've hurt her pretty badly,' said Kildare. 'I'm sorry that I wasn't here to take the whole brunt of it.'

'Hurt her?' said Lamont. 'I tell you, for that girl I've—but I won't talk about it. It drives me mad. And in the end what has she done? She's betrayed me! With her little doctor—for my own good—she's stabbed me in the back. When I think that she was consenting to this—'

'She knew nothing about it. She didn't even know what was in the injection.'

'Kildare,' said Lamont, 'the truth is that I want to be fair. I detest brawling and wrangling. I'll admit that you've hit me a good, hard blow. But you see it hasn't knocked me down. I'm on my feet again.

'I suppose Messenger is a lost opportunity. And furthermore, I suppose a rumor already is spreading about me. Willoughby and the rest—they're beginning to spread the word that I'm a poor incompetent, a weakling who gets a cold in the head and can't toe the mark—'

He broke off, groaning, his head bent far back in an agony of shame.

'I'll still take my chance,' he said, 'or what's left of it.'

'I hope you will—in the right way,' said Kildare.

'And what's the right way, my friend?'

'The slow way, for you,' said Kildare. 'You'd better take everything easily. Instead of being eloquent with other people and arguing your points, better write them out and let it go at that. Personal contacts always cause friction, and that's an exhausting thing. You must not be exhausted, Douglas.'

'I'd better sit still the rest of my days, then?'

'By all means.'

'What the devil are you talking about, Kildare?'

'I can't tell you.'

'The fact is, Kildare, that you're trying to make capital out of my extraordinary exhaustion of yesterday.'

'It isn't the exhaustion that interested me,' said Kildare.

'Ah. No?'

'It's the cause of it,' said Kildare.

'And what is the cause, if you please? ... But why do I ask you? I know what it is. The rush and strain of this crazy city, of course.'

'No,' said Kildare.

'Come, come, then. Out with it.'

'I need observation of you before I can be sure. I want to persuade you to take this prescription that I've brought.'

'And sleep some more?'

'It would make you sleep—for one thing.'

'I suspected that. Now, Jimmy, let me be perfectly frank with you. I have work ahead of me that will take every hour of my day. I have ideas to clear up that will use every scruple of my energy; and I simply haven't time for you now.'

'I have to tell you the nature of the disease, then,' said Kildare. 'I'm sorry. I wanted to get you on a regime that would help you without telling you the entire truth.'

'A shocking truth, I suppose?' said Lamont, coldly.

'It's hard on you,' said Kildare. 'But these alternations of a clear brain and an inert brain—up in the clouds and then down in the hollows—doesn't remind you of anything in the way of disease, Douglas?'

'Not a thing. Now, my dear fellow, let me warn you of something. I've heard Mary talk about your miracles as a diagnostician, and all that. But the fact is that you've made no thorough examination of me. You've felt my pulse, and that's all. So I'm afraid that I must warn you from the beginning that I won't be very interested in what you have to say.'

'I think you will when I tell you that it's epilepsy that I'm talking about,' said Kildare.

The hand of Lamont jumped to his face. He rubbed it hard across his eyes. Then he stared at Kildare.

'Epilepsy? Epilepsy?' he repeated.

'You made me come out with it. It's a disease that people are terribly afraid of, of course. But I can tell you things about its real nature and the possibilities of control...'

'Epilepsy?' repeated Lamont again.

He surprised Kildare by putting back his head and laughing heartily.

'You've come to the wrong fellow with this silly song and dance,' he said. 'Epilepsy? People falling in faints and fits? Let me tell you that I've never had a fit in my life. I think that does in your argument pretty thoroughly doesn't it?'

'You have the petit mal,' said Kildare. 'And I also think that you have the grand mal.'

'And the fits?' demanded Lamont.

'At night, as you sleep, the aura comes to you. That's why you wake up and find yourself thinking surprising thoughts.'

'You mean that epilepsy is an inspiration?'

'Not usually,' said Kildare. 'But the aura often gives a sense of ascending to a height, of looking down at life, of understanding the

119

whole scheme of things.'

'So that my project, for instance, is simply the idea of a diseased brain?'

'I don't say that. There have been some eminent people who suffered badly from the disease, you know. There was Mahomet; there was Caesar.'

'Epileptics? My dear Jimmy, you're determined to astonish me?'

'I'm sorry,' said Kildare.

'If epilepsy can produce genius, why don't we *breed* for the disease?'

'Because perhaps only one in a hundred thousand reacts so favorably. And even in these, the mind is apt to shrivel and die away. You see? The aura has come over you when you're asleep. That would be the grand mal, and that's the reason you haven't been observed in a fall and a fit. The petit mal is so brief an attack, with you, that you hardly notice its passing except that there's sometimes a brief lacuna in your memory of a conversation. Isn't that true?'

'Kildare, I sympathize with your energy. But I'm sorry for the way you waste your time. Epilepsy may seem a clever idea. But I have work, Kildare, and I must do it. Tomorrow night I go to see Messenger's experts, it appears. And up to that time, nobody can prescribe for me. Not afterward, either. Kildare, can't you see that your curious invention is of no importance

120

whatever to me?'

'I can understand that,' agreed Kildare. He in turn faced the little window that looked on the still, daylit street. 'But let me give you a proof that will take you to a full understanding of what the thing is. In other words, if we don't fight to cure epilepsy, I must tell you that it generally involves a serious and progressive weakening of the brain.'

'I suppose so. I dare say,' muttered Lamont. 'But great Scott, man! Do you think that I'll listen to you or any other man until you've proved what's wrong with me, definitely, with laboratory reports or what you please.'

'You're largely an eater of salad and vegetables, aren't you?' said Kildare, shifting the subject suddenly.

'Yes. That's right. I suppose Mary told you that?'

'Douglas, if you'll take dinner with me tonight, I'll promise you that you'll develop the disease at the table. If you'll dine with me at six-thirty, you'll have a stroke of the grand mal by eight-thirty...'

'Hello!' said Douglas.

He began to smile. His surety was so great that this challenge seemed more whimsical than real to him.

'Have a cook slip a little stuff into my food, eh?' he asked.

'We'll eat wherever you please—so long as steak is one of the parts of your order. A good steak and a few glasses of beer?'

'Very well,' said Douglas. 'Why, there's to be a little mystery in this, after all. I can pick any place I wish?'

'It had better be in the safety of your own room,' said Kildare.

'This is the damnedest thing I've ever heard of,' said Douglas. 'At six-thirty I'll expect you here. It's like witchcraft and the Dark Ages. I feel as if I were going to meet Houdini, not the young doctor at all!'

CHAPTER FOURTEEN

EAT—AND KNOW TERROR

It made a strange occasion. Mary Lamont, who knew nothing of the peculiar point involved in the meeting, was childishly delighted when she knew that Kildare was to be alone with her brother that evening.

'I know how I left him,' she kept repeating. 'I don't see how you talked your way back to a friendship with him so quickly. It's like black witchcraft, Jimmy.'

He remembered, afterwards, that they both had used the word 'Witchcraft.' It was one of a good many details that stuck in his mind in the time to come, in the long bitterness that was to follow.

But he found Lamont comparatively cheerful that evening. He had had a good day with his work. He had written his speech, reviewed his answers for the great occasion. And tomorrow night he was to meet Messenger with the experts reassembled.

'There may have been less harm done by that postponement than I thought at first,' he said when Kildare came into the room that evening. 'Perhaps you did me a favor—and were paid back by a thorough damning. And by the way, I've telephoned to Mary, and I think she's happier. The trouble is that I get into states of rather a high tension. You'll forgive me for it, Jimmy, won't you?'

This cheerfulness and friendliness astonished Kildare. But there is nothing like successful work to take the black blood out of a man, of course.

Douglas Lamont was as alert as a child, and as excited over the experiment. His surety that Kildare was totally wrong was absolute. He had arranged to have the meal served up from the wretched kitchen of his hotel in his room.

'There are rules to this game, Jimmy,' he said. 'You'll be served at the table, here, and I'll have my steak in this far corner by the window. I'll have the window open, too.

There may be some little device of yours that could be brought into play, and we'll protect ourselves against it.

'But actually, don't you think it's good sense to give up this tomfoolery? It was a leap in the dark, on your part. You don't want to stay by it, do you?'

'Yes. I want to stay by it,' said Kildare.

So they sat in the opposite corners of the room in order that Kildare could not tamper with the food that was served to his host. The steaks were too thin, too well done, too greasy.

But Douglas paid no attention to the quality of his food. His mind already was flying forward toward the execution of the great project again, and that happy time when city workers no longer would sleep in the concrete cells of apartment houses.

'If this food could do me harm, why hasn't it harmed me in the past?' he asked Kildare.

'Since you started working on the project,' said Kildare, 'tell me what your diet has been, as a rule?'

'Why, food hasn't interested me a great deal,' answered Douglas. 'A salad and a light sandwich, for instance; plenty of calories in that sort of thing; and the saving in time is of course enormous. The advantage of letting the mind flow straightforward from the moment a man gets up to the moment he goes to bed again—the value of that hasn't been pointed out enough. I could claim it almost as my discovery. For the mind never grows tired, Jimmy. The body, yes. Cramped positions at work, and that sort of thing, will weary a man. But not the use of the mind. Can you agree?'

'So your meals were picked up as you worked—an apple, a glass of milk, a sandwich, a salad, eh?'

'That's right.'

'Well,' said Kildare, 'it's not eight-thirty. We're taking this pretty lightly, Douglas.'

'You'll see how totally wrong you are,' answered Lamont. 'And a light attitude is the right one. There's only one thing that I'd be serious about. Mary is never to know that you had this suspicion about me?'

'Entirely right,' said Kildare.

'Good!' said Lamont, and a moment later he was off on the project once more, and the incalculable value of a simpler life. Not simple in fact, but simple in its stimuli. Children play at make-believe; men should work at creation. It is not what fills us from the outside, whether it be in sound or sights, but what we make grow within us, to be ready to pour forth as an original expression. The project would give this talent back to man, as nature had intended him to be.

Eight-fifteen and eight-thirty passed. Kildare, listening to the chime of a neighboring bell that struck the hours, watched the passage of the moments with a keen consciousness; but Lamont was still abroad in his visions when he noticed, suddenly, that it was almost nine.

He made a great point of it, showing Kildare his watch and even ringing up to make sure of the time.

'Is that the end of your idea?' he asked.

Kildare, still considering him with an almost reluctant air, could not help smiling.

'I've just begun to hope that I'm wrong,' he said.

'Of course you're wrong,' answered Lamont. 'But—By the way, it's getting a bit chilly here, isn't it?'

'I haven't noticed that,' said Kildare.

'I mean, close to the floor—a draught of some kind?'

Kildare stood up. He said: 'A chill rising from your feet toward your knees?'

'Why, as a mater of fact, that's the sensation.'

'As if a cold mist were creeping up through you?'

'That's it, also. Like a wind blowing up through the body. I don't remember anything like that, except in dreams.'

'Douglas,' said Kildare, 'lie down and stretch out. It's the aura coming.'

'Aura? What sort of nonsense is that?'

'It's the first sign of the stroke in epilepsy of some forms. Lie down, Douglas, please.'

But Lamont stood up from his chair.

'Above the knees, and rising into my body; blowing toward my brain, Jimmy! God help me, do you mean that it's the true symptom?'

'It's the true symptom,' said Kildare. 'Get to the bed and stretch out, Douglas. Don't—'

He had started to approach Lamont. He had to jump to get to him in time as the body of the man went rigid and toppled sidewise to the floor. He fell like a log into the arms of Kildare.

He was so starved and wasted that Kildare lifted him with ease and laid him on the bed. He had brought with him the necessaries.

And after the first injection, Lamont began to come out of the fit. His head, pulling back against the straining cords of his neck, gradually straightened. His lips, stretched back into a horrible grin, slowly softened once more; and now the eyes opened with a gradual return of sense revealed in them.

It was half an hour later before he roused from that semi-coma.

Kildare, seated close beside the bed, held the cold hand in his strong grip. There was bewilderment in the face of Lamont, then fear, and finally utter sorrow. Through all of those changes he did not speak.

Kildare said: 'Will you let me talk to you about it a little?'

'What's the use of the talk?' asked Lamont. 'I know what happens.'

'Tell me, then,' said Kildare.

'The brain dries up like a dead apple. A man doesn't dare take two steps away from his house. Even if he stands in his room he may be struck down like a piece of falling wood. My God, Jimmy, I wish—'

'That you'd never met me?'

'You see, I'm already talking like the fool I'll disintegrate into.'

'There's no reason for that.'

'Admit that there's no cure.'

'There are ways of arresting the progress, old fellow. You only need to play everything safe.'

'This is all truth that you intend to tell me?'

'All truth. Not a word exaggerated.'

'Go on, then,' said Lamont. 'It's been a hard thing to watch, hasn't it?'

'No. Not hard. I've seen it before.'

'Your collar's wilted. The color's washed out of your face. You look like wet clay. Gray clay. And still you say it wasn't hard to watch?'

'Think of yourself, man, not about what it means to me.'

'And Mary? She's to know nothing about it?'

'Not now. Not a word, just now.'

'Good,' sighed Lamont. 'But what

128

happens to me is nothing. It's the project that counts, Jimmy. Tell me what I'm to do about it?'

'You've got to live on a careful regime,' said Kildare. 'Think of yourself as a tree: A big pine full of resin, you understand?'

'I'll keep the picture in mind. What does it mean?'

'It means that there's material in you to feed a small flame, a candle flame, for years. You see?'

Lamont nodded, carefully attentive to Kildare's words, examining them for some thread of hope. He said:

'Exactly. But not a big blaze of light?'

'Not a big blaze of light. You could burn up in an hour, Douglas. And that's what we've got to watch against. No big excitements. Everything should be calm and quiet.'

'The project?' said Lamont, lifting himself on his elbows, with his haunted eyes giving the great question to Kildare.

'You can carry on with it.'

Lamont dropped back on the bed and groaned with relief.

'You can carry on with it,' continued Kildare. 'But not so actively. You can't make stump speeches or hammer your points home in arguments. But you can write a book about it.'

'Write a book!' cried Lamont. 'I might as

well dig a trench and bury it in the ground. That's what books are. Cemeteries where ideas are buried. Listen to me, Jimmy. *This* is the time when the project is needed, and when people realize that something like it has to be done. Here's Messenger lined up with his three experts. If I could convince them, everything would be easy. He'd push the thing through.'

Kildare spoke calmly.

'Write out the main points. I'll take Messenger the letter and explain that you can't see anyone.'

'No one? Do you mean that I have to live like a thing in a cave?'

'By degrees we'll give you a freer and freer life. But we have to go by degrees.'

'I tell you, Jimmy,' said Lamont, 'that unless I can press the argument home, the project goes by the board. It's lost. It's a forgotten dream. It's a mere nothingness!'

'Hush,' said Kildare. 'Lie quietly for a moment, and we'll talk the thing through. Everything that can be done, believe me I'll try to do it. We're shoulder to shoulder, and we'll try to win out.'

'Do you mean, Jimmy, that you believe in me and in the project?'

'I believe in you and in the project,' said Kildare, solemnly, like a man making a declaration of faith.

CHAPTER FIFTEEN

THIS IS MY BROTHER

Twice the next day, Kildare got off for brief visits to Douglas Lamont. He was able to say to Mary: 'He's resting easily. But I wouldn't call on him. Not just now. He's perfectly tranquil and he's all clear about you, Mary. He's dropped all his wild ideas about treachery.'

'Even *I* would be too much for him?' she said.

'You know how it is,' said Kildare. 'A man comes to the end of his tether and doesn't realize how gone he is until he starts relaxing. Then the weakness comes over him—in a wave.'

'And the second meeting with Mr. Messenger? That has to go by the board, too?'

'There'll be plenty of other chances for that,' he told her.

'It only makes me wonder,' she said. 'When I think what a tiger he was, Jimmy! I just wonder that he can be patient now!'

He looked away from her, remembering the empty, dead eyes that had looked up from the bed at him, this day. Well, 'patience' was one word for it, though despair might have been a better one. And it was not altogether a lie to say that Douglas was 'resting easily.'

He went on, cheerfully: 'It was simply a matter of being frank with him, and pointing out that he must give up the powerhouse tactics that he's been pursuing. The idea of a battleship's engine put in a ferry boat—that seemed to make it clear to him that his power was shaking him to pieces. You see? Too much vibration for the size of the boat. He grew entirely sensible.'

He winced just a trifle when he said this, recalling how Douglas Lamont had shrunk as the bludgeoning of medical common sense was given to him. Kildare could not tell that the accurate eye of Mary Lamont had registered the pain with which he spoke.

'The main thing now,' said Kildare, 'is for him to be quiet and watch his diet. No meat for a while. Light, simple things, and all that. But he'll build up fast, I hope.'

'And the drinking?' she asked.

She had a way of standing close to him, looking up to study his face. She was doing it now, with a religious intensity.

'Of course, the drinking was bad. Not that he did much of it. No moral danger, as they say. But he thought it was a crutch that he could lean on, you know.'

He went off, turning after a few steps to smile at her.

That struck her harder than anything else. It was not his way to consider her very much, except in emergencies. The rest of the time he went his own way with his head down, like a bulldog. The pause, the turning, the smile seemed to her typical of the Jimmy Kildare who, in a pinch, could be so filled with tenderness. There *was* a crisis, then, after all.

The beat of her heart was hurried. The old breathlessness returned on her. With every step she made down the hospital corridor there increased in her mind the certainty that Kildare had hidden something important about her brother.

Young Dr. Bixby came up from behind her with a rapid stride.

'Hai!' he said, going by.

'Hai—wait a minute!' she called after him. He slowed up as she joined him.

'I want an answer to a riddle,' she said.

'Medical?'

'Yes. Lots of phenobarbital and no meat—that sort of thing?'

'Phenobarbital—and low protein ... Why, that sounds like something serious. Let's see,' said Bixby. 'Ah, I remember now. It sounds like—that's it—epilepsy! That's what it's apt to be.'

'Ah! Thanks a lot,' she said.

He went on, for her feet had slowed to a totter and then to a complete halt. She put her hand against the wall and remembered to breathe deeply. It seemed to her that beyond the wall, in every room, there were housed secrets hostile to her.

It was the end of her day, at any rate, and she could give thanks for that. It enabled her to go to her room, and Molly Cavendish, the head nurse, walked up the stairs with her with a man's large, capable stride that made her skirts swish noisily.

'So you're dying by inches, still?' said Molly Cavendish. 'Now, there's something I thank God for, and that's the fact that I've left damned nonsense twenty-five years behind me. I used to die, too. But after a while you find out that there's nothing worth dying for. Is it any better to be the way I am? I don't know. *You* think that the yellow stuff is all gold; and I know that it's only gilding. It's better to be a happy fool than a sad old woman, maybe. But when I see the white in your face, darling, I can't tell whether I want to spank you or love you.'

At the door of Mary's room she paused and said: 'It's that young Kildare, of course?'

'No. Not really. Not at all,' said Mary.

'But you're admitting that there's only a sick, sick heart in you? And there's no place to turn?'

'No.'

'And even if you could have the whole world, would you want it?'

134

'No,' said Mary.

'Well, then there's Kildare in it somewhere,' said Molly Cavendish, 'and I've half a mind to find him and tell him a few home truths.'

'No, please, please!'

'Why shouldn't I?'

'You won't do it? You won't say a word?'

'All right,' said Molly Cavendish, 'but let me tell you something: there's damned few things in the world that straight talk won't make come all right in the end.'

She went off down the hall with her heavy footfall. Mary, alone in the waiting stillness of her small room, knew that she could not endure it for a single hour. She bathed, changed, and went out into the twilight bound for her brother's hotel.

It was dark when she reached it. The door was strangely ajar when she knocked at it. A maid with towels over her arm came to open for her.

'The gentleman's out,' said she.

Mary looked past her to a service tray on the table. What held her eyes was the remnant of a steak: a chunk of fat and gristle with some shred of meat adhering. It was an ugly thing to look at, a small, ugly thing; and it had ten added meanings to her since Bixby had suggested something.

According to Kildare, Douglas was stretched on his bed, resting, relaxed, preparing himself for only small exertions. According to Kildare, Douglas had given up his appointment for this evening with Messenger for a second time. According to facts, Douglas was not in his room at all!

It was not epilepsy, of course. That dreadful sickness of her heart was foolish. It was not epilepsy. A man who knows he has a thing like that obeys doctor's orders as she would obey an angel from heaven. And here was Douglas out on the city.

At the drugstore she telephoned to the Messenger house, saying: 'This is Dr. Kildare's office calling. Is Mr. Douglas Lamont expected there this evening?'

'Mr. Lamont has been here for an hour already,' said the butler. 'The gentlemen having been here for at least an hour. Any message from the doctor?'

'No message,' she said.

She was smiling as she reached the pavement again and there were tears of happiness in her eyes. After all, she must learn to take her suspicions less seriously, she told herself. She had been trying to read things into Kildare's face and voice, and his parting smile.

As a matter of fact, what she had learned from Bixby was the mere happen-chance that seems to fit in with facts, now and then. But, really, Douglas was exactly as Kildare had represented him—spent, exhausted.

And a day's rest in bed had done so much for him that he had felt entirely equal to going to Messenger's house and arguing his points with the experts.

She walked on, too happy to know where she was going except that she was moving cross-town, toward one of the brilliantly lighted avenues.

There was only one point that she could not reason out and explain. That non-protein diet was what stopped her. For she could not help remembering the steak that had made a dinner for Douglas.

Suppose that it *were* that horrible name—epilepsy—that concerned her brother? She tried to remember what she could of the disease. Usually it was accompanied by mental decay, longer and more severe spastic fits, and could lead to death; certainly led to a tortured and abbreviated life.

But there were rare cases. Medicine knew very little about them because they rarely came to hospitals or asked for treatment. They were the men and the women in whom epilepsy appeared as a sudden enormous brightening of the flame, interspersed with periods of excessive dullness.

She remembered learning about Danton, great and terrible as a conflagration even among the wild figures of the French Revolution. He had loomed in Paris time and again to make tremendous pronouncements that changed the fate of the world.

And then he would disappear out to a quiet little country house. There nothing could move him, not even threats of personal danger. And finally he would appear again, always briefly, always a dazzling light.

When the Allies poured toward Paris, it was Danton who taught France how to meet them and cried for *'de l'audace, et encore de l'audace, et toujours de l'audace!'* But hardly a moment later, and he was gone back to the green peace and quiet of his countryside. Was not the terrible Danton an epileptic of that singular variety, like a variable star that now is brilliant, now dim?

And there were others, whose flame came and went more swiftly. There were Caesar, Mahomet. Perhaps that most eloquent of Englishmen, that empire-builder, Chatham, was afflicted by epilepsy when, during his second administration, he sat in his country estate unable to meet even his dearest friends, unable to lift a hand in the crises of his country's affairs.

These things came to her dimly, and others more clearly out of the past, but they were more hearsay than fact. What troubled her was the realization that Douglas had varied between a penetrating eagerness of mind and a sluggish dullness.

And if diet controlled the disease—if indeed he *were* epileptic and the diet controlled it—might he not have induced the aura by ordering the very food which Kildare had forbidden him?

The terror caught her by the throat. She walked on more rapidly, realizing that all the while she had been bent on reaching the house of Paul Messenger in her subconscious mind. She saw it now looming in the next block, and the sight of it reassured her subtly and completely.

She walked down the block in front of it, paused a moment at the corner and turned back again. She was nearly in front of it when the front door of the house opened and Douglas Lamont stood at the head of the steps.

The brilliant hall-lights streamed out around him. He was not alone. Paul Messenger himself was in the open doorway, and three other men surrounded Douglas. But he was the dominant figure, though he was smaller than any of the others. He stood out from them like a Napoleon surrounded by marshals. They were inclining their heads toward him, watching him, listening to his words.

She could hear him say: 'Ah, Willoughby, you're the one I was particularly afraid of.'

And a tall, leaning, studious figure bowed toward Douglas, saying: 'The fact is that

139

your idea has a double value, Lamont. In the first place, it is what every man in the world wants to believe in; in the second place you're poet enough to make every man think that it can be done; and economist enough to spike the guns of the enemy, as you've spiked ours tonight.'

They came on down the steps. Douglas had turned to say goodnight again to big Paul Messenger, who stood above them, radiant. Now he was passing down along with the others, and they attended him, it seemed to her happy, tear-filled eyes, like lesser creatures around one divinely chosen.

This was his great moment and he had made the best of it. Perhaps he would fit into one of those highest niches which are reserved in the history of mankind for the great geniuses, the great benefactors.

He stood on the lowest step, now, and suddenly seemed to grow higher. She saw the men on his right and left carry him by the arms. He had stiffened, his head thrown far back, his arms thrusting out into crooked, stiff, rigid positions, like the arms of a statue awkwardly poised. She could see the distention of the cords in his throat. A voice that seemed to come from the mouth of a beast groaned aloud. And then he fell.

CHAPTER SIXTEEN

FAREWELL TO LOVE

They caught at him. They prevented him from striking the sidewalk but before they could lift him again, she had her arms around him.

It was like embracing a figure of wood. Paul Messenger was running down the steps. She stood up. She heard her voice saying, calmly: 'Call for Dr. Kildare at the Blair General Hospital, and carry him back into the house.'

They obeyed her. They did not exclaim, these men of mind, but each gave his attention studiously to the work in hand. Somehow Paul Messenger managed to take the whole weight into his arms. He carried the trembling body back into his house.

There was his daughter, Nancy, coming hurrying. She had a quick smile of recognition for Mary Lamont. And then Mary's voice was giving directions again—to prepare a hot bath and get him into it, and above all to get Dr. Kildare, quickly, quickly!

They carried Douglas up the stairs. As they went, she could hear the voice of Nancy crying at a telephone: 'Jimmy, this is Nancy … Jimmy dear, come quickly—jump as fast

as you can! Douglas Lamont has collapsed
... Yes, yes, he's here at Father's house ... It
seems to be a fit of some sort...'

She followed the body of Douglas, frozen
as if by death. And was it not in fact a death
that had occurred? All that happened around
her became fixed, static, as if a slow moving
picture projected the images upon the screen
of her mind.

She never could forget the silly
Gainsborough, golden and blue and foolish,
that hung in the upper hall, or, in a niche
hollowed in the wall, a Greek head
remodeled by some patient Roman copyist.
Twenty centuries had turned the marble to
pale gold, but the statue had been hardly
used. The nose was half chipped away, the
back of the head was gone, and great
excoriations ran up one side of the face. Half
her smile had disappeared, and yet the smile
was there, and the grace, and the girlish
sweetness which somehow shone more
clearly through the torment and the
disfigurement and the long, long rain of
years. It seemed to Mary Lamont an
exquisite distillation of her own agony, a sort
of fellow sorrow which she could take to her
heart.

Down the upper hall the deep nap of the
carpet muffled all footfalls to whisperings. In
this hush she followed Douglas to a grave.
Perhaps he would not die; but it was death

for her, death for the children that should be born to her, death to all the years of her life that were to have been spent with Kildare.

Two times the blow had fallen in one family, and that was enough. Her uncle had died in an institution; and now her own brother was tainted in the brain. The whiz of the arrow had gone just past her cheek. When she had reached the same age—who could tell what she would be?

And there was Kildare to be wounded by the same stroke. *He* would not shrink back from such a danger to their life together, but he would have no children, of course. He never would speak a reproach; he never would permit himself even inwardly to regret. That was the stuff he was made of, that champion of lost causes.

Time went vaguely past her. Her hands were occupied now. Her voice giving directions. All the other people were gone except the great and terrible Willoughby, he of the baby face and the gigantic brow; and there was stalwart Paul Messenger, and lovely Nancy.

What had been done could hardly be wrong; and now they had Douglas in a bed where the fresh attacks of convulsion stretched him again and again, as if on a rack. Froth kept coming to his lips, a blood-stained froth. His eyes, partially open, and his hard-drawn mouth, seemed to express resistance to the torment. He was like a picture of one about to scream.

'It's going to be all right,' said Nancy.

For an instant full consciousness rushed back on Mary and she looked into the eyes of the other girl, and saw her moving in deep space and time, surrounded by wealth and love and children and happiness so still and perfect that it would be like quiet music.

'All right, did you say?' asked Mary, and she saw Nancy shrink. There was a perfect comprehension in this girl, at least.

She said: 'Jimmy will make everything right, Mary. Jimmy always makes everything right. You know how he is and what he can do.'

'Yes. I know,' said Mary. 'This time he has a perfect chance to throw his *own* life away. It's what he's made for, isn't it? You couldn't know him; you couldn't look at him, without understanding that he'd have no luck in the end.'

Her voice surprised her own ears, it was so curiously level and easily modulated, as if she were a teacher pointing out a medical instance in a classroom, or a lecturer illustrating a point of character in someone long dead. She saw the head of Nancy bow.

Afterward, Nancy said something to her father; and from that point forward the eye of Messenger dwelt on her from time to time with a profound, gloomy understanding and sympathy. *They* knew that she had accepted the emptiness of the future, and they knew that there was no other honorable thing for her to do.

She had to leave Jimmy. She had to drive him away in such a fashion that he never would come near her again. In some way, she would manage to work out a scheme that would appear sound. There was Douglas to take care of. That was to be her life work.

That was to be everything.

She saw it all clearly. It would be a life in miniature. Bitterness by degrees would pinch her mouth and harden her eyes.

Kildare suddenly was in the room. Nancy Messenger was kissing him. If only Nancy would keep the tears out of her eyes! For there must be no tears now. All was to be calm, stone-calm and steady forever. She could thank God that Kildare himself was as undemonstrative as a rock.

He was a little pale; but then his color rarely was good. The darkness of continual exhaustion always was thumbed in around his eyes. But he was steady; he was like a rock. There never was a tremor of his hands.

He was opening his medical kit while he was on his way across the room. A moment later he was breaking the ampule of phenobarbital. He took the whole of it into his hypodermic; three whole grains he gave to Douglas in the arm. Then he sat down to watch.

She became aware of time and events once more. It was a classical condition of epilepsy, the true status epilepticus that kills through exhaustion unless the patient is brought out before many hours.

She began to use a towel to wipe away the sweat from the face and throat of Douglas, and to clear his mouth of the blood-stained froth. Kildare, hooking a stethoscope around his neck, listened from time to time to the heart: to the ventricles, to the auricles, and then back to the big laboring ventricles. Now he took the pulse to see how the beats were coming through.

It was as impossible to read his mind as if he had been a statue. She began to massage, softly, the neck cords, and looked to Kildare for permission. He nodded.

She did not exist for him, she knew, except as a machine. He was suspended in space. There was no room around him, no people. There was only his patient. She had seen him, so many times before in exactly this state of suspension, pouring all his mind, all his energy into a patient; as if from some store of electrical energy he were able to give back the vital strength to the sick.

There was one peculiarity about him: he nearly always had a finger on the pulse, or resting lightly on the arm of the patient, as if instinctively he needed that physical contact

146

and received through it those impalpable impressions, those swift, dim messages which come only to a very great doctor.

Some people, when they talked about him in the hospital—and they always were talking about the rising of this bright, new star—declared that his skin was too thin. He could not continue giving his own vitality to every patient that came into his hands. But she knew they were wrong. The more he gave, the more there was to be given.

Douglas began to roll his eyes. They turned wildly to the right, then to the left. Then back they turned, the lids wide open, the eyeball distended, with the little red arteries coming into visibility.

When sense goes out of the eyes, a man seems to become a mere beast. And so it was with Douglas. He was not her brother. He was merely a sufferer for whom, with the passage of every moment, her hope grew less and less.

It was midnight, suddenly. For hours he had been lying there receiving shock after shock of the convulsions. Usually epileptics turned rigid with the fit, then relaxed; and the convulsion might come again later, when nature had restored some strength to the body. But this was one long, long tension which, in the end, must snap the thread of life.

It was wonderful that Douglas had

endured as long as this. It seemed clear to her that without the touch of Kildare upon him he would have died long hours ago. And love for the young doctor burst upward, suddenly, from her heart. It pressed like an exploding force against her teeth. She set them harder.

The wild impulse receded, died away. She was vastly grateful that the all-seeing eye of Kildare had not fallen upon her at that moment. It never would happen again. It never would come to her again. At the source, in the heart itself, she would learn how to control and kill every one of these tremendous outgoings.

Time takes care of such matters. There would come a day when she would be able to talk, calmly, of the time when she had been a hospital nurse. She could hear herself telling some faintly interested companion how she had seen genius come to the Blair General Hospital, and how he had been looked on askance, and how he had persisted in his bulldog ways, making his own independent diagnoses, clinging to them in spite of the devil and all authority, again and again on the verge of expulsion, again and again reaccepted, until at last the strange news was abroad in the whole great institution that a genius, a creature of compacted and brilliant light, was among them.

By that time he would be 'the celebrated

Doctor Kildare,' 'The greatest diagnostician since the death of famous Doctor Gillespie.' News reporters are learning how to write about scientists of genius. They would learn to write about Kildare in the same manner. He would be up there for the world to admire; and all the while he would carry on with that strange humility which she knew so well, that selfless purpose which he had been born to and which he inherited again from the great Gillespie.

He, at least, would never forget her. There was no forgetfulness in that brain of his.

Now she heard Messenger saying: 'Mr. Willoughby, don't you think you had better go and get some rest?'

She glanced quickly around the room. It was two in the morning. Nancy still was there, fetching and carrying when anything was needed. Paul Messenger was there. So was the baby face, the huge, smooth forehead of the famous Willoughby.

She heard Willoughby answering: 'May I ask the doctor a question?'

'Certainly, Mr. Willoughby.'

'Doctor, is not your patient in considerable danger?' asked Willoughby.

'He is in danger,' said Kildare, without visible emotion.

'In that case,' said Willoughby, 'if it is permitted, I should like to remain with my colleague.' He added, rather dreamily: 'We

149

have not his like in the world, you know. Doctor, may I ask you what hopes there may be, and to what the seizure may be attributed?'

Kildare did not turn his head. He seemed to be speaking to the unconscious man on the bed as he said: 'This man could have kept a reasonable degree of health and safety if he had been willing to live quietly; if he had been willing to move the mountain a grain of sand at a time. But he was afraid that his idea would die unless he fought for it now. He knew that he was risking his life. He chose to risk it.'

Willoughby stood up from his chair. He seemed about to speak, then changed his mind and sank into the chair slowly again.

Messenger said in a moved voice: 'I hope that his work does not have to fail without him, Mr. Willoughby?'

There was a moment of silence then, and Messenger seemed almost frightened.

'Perhaps not,' said Willoughby. 'But he is the torch that set us on fire. We are cold souls. Can we pass along the fire that was in him? Can we make people venture their money, their souls?'

'We can try,' said Messenger.

'We can,' answered Willoughby, 'and we shall!'

Kildare, his finger on the pulse having discovered something, put the stethoscope suddenly over the heart of Douglas. He listened intently.

She thought: '*God have mercy!*'

Kildare glanced quickly up at her, and she knew that she had uttered her thought aloud. Kildare said, in that calm, familiar voice, which always was deepened and enriched by the great crisis: 'There is still a good chance. There is a spinal puncture to relieve the intracranial pressure.'

Her cold hands assisted in turning Douglas, in baring his back, in sterilizing a place for the needle. She saw the liquid drawn off in the syringe. The back was covered, the body turned again. And Kildare once more listened with the stethoscope, intently.

After a moment he glanced up at her from out of that hidden world whose mysteries he knew so well. He looked at her and one of his rare smiles came and went.

A groaning breath of relief passed her lips. This was the reprieve for which she had stopped hoping. And almost at once the tension commenced to relax in the cords of the throat. The breathing of Douglas grew stertorous, then more normal. The wooden rigidity passed from his body. His eyes closed, then opened suddenly with clear consciousness in them again, at last.

His voice said, faintly but very clearly: 'For the sake of the poor, for the sake of the handless, helpless poor, for the sake of the inert and prostrate minds, gentlemen, let us make the great attempt and trust in God. Let us...'

The voice trailed away. He slept.

'We shall,' said Willoughby's hushed voice. 'We shall trust in God!'

Someone was sobbing very quietly. That was Nancy. And then, by a miracle, Mary found that she was alone in the room with Kildare and the sleeping man.

It was much later. The dawn was beginning to finger the big windows. And she had returned from a long, sad trek of the imagination across weary continents of thoughts.

Kildare stood up and she rose also, instinctively. He was very tired. His lips fumbled the words as he said: 'He can lead a life that will have to be very quiet at first. But he can increase his activity by degrees. I've written out the diet and the prescription for the medicine. He can be moved from here later on today, or perhaps early tomorrow. Telephone to me if there is any bad change. I think that's all.'

She saw that the time had come to strike the blow. She could sever the mooring line and cast herself adrift from him forever. Kind explanations never would do, with him. He simply would insist. He would beat down resistance, finally with ease. It was

152

with a sharp edge that she must deal with him, and nothing else.

'You've been very kind and efficient,' she said.

He glanced sharply at her, frowning, bewildered by her tone.

'But let's be frank. Isn't that the best way? Of course I know that you could have prevented all this, if you'd chosen to.'

'Prevented—if I'd chosen?' he echoed, helplessly.

She opened the door for him.

'Instead of that, you've let his life become a ruin. And what are you or a thousand like you compared with one mind like this?'

He walked past her into the hall.

'You're tired and a little wild, Mary,' he said. 'I'll talk to you later on.'

Without a reply, she closed the door on him, heavily. And, having closed it, her body leaned against it, her face in the hollow of her arm as she sobbed. If he came back now, he would understand everything at a glance. But he did not come back. She prayed that the doorknob would turn, but it remained inert under her hand.

CHAPTER SEVENTEEN

TELL SALLY

Kildare, back at the hospital, still shaking his head to clear it of the strange nightmare impression which Mary had left in him, passed a softly singing voice at the telephone board.

'Good morning, Dr. Kildare!' called Sally. She glanced around her to make sure that there was no one within hearing distance. 'How is everything, doc?'

'Everything's all right,' said Kildare. 'And how about Joe?'

'This is his last day on the ambulance,' she said. 'Oh, I've made him swear higher than a stack of Bibles. Get the promises when you can. That's my idea. We're gunna be so happy. The big mug! We're gunna be so happy. Thanks to you, doc!'

He went up to bed, set his alarm clock, and fell heavily asleep. It seemed hardly five minutes before the speaker was saying: 'Dr. Kildare, wanted in Dr. Gillespie's office ... Dr. Kildare wanted in Dr. Gillespie's office.'

He stumbled into his white clothes and went down to the waiting line. He carried with him a vague sense of disastrous defeat; it was only later that he remembered the words of Mary, but they were too strange for credence.

The first shock came when he rang the nursing home and found that Mary Lamont had resigned her position.

The second blow was when Molly Cavendish, that afternoon, stopped in his office to say: 'So you let her go, did you? You kept at her until her heart was gone out of her, and then you let her slip away?'

Her face was grim.

'But she's not away,' said Kildare. 'The fact is...'

'Argue with your grandmother, not with me,' said Molly Cavendish, and slammed out of the room.

He rang Paul Messenger's house then.

She was not there. She had called in an outside doctor who gave permission to move Douglas, who was greatly recovered after his sleep. An ambulance had called. The Messengers did not know the address to which she had taken her brother.

After that, Kildare was a serious man. Hardly an hour later a special delivery was brought to him, a little packet containing a brief note from Mary Lamont. It read:

DEAR JIMMY:
The fact is that we'd never be able to forget what has happened to Douglas. You'd never forget and I'd never forgive.

So let's agree to stop trying. We've never done a very good job of life, even in the planning of it. So what chance would there have been in tackling the reality together?

I'm sending back your letters. All three of them. Certainly you weren't inspired to any great eloquence by this girl, were you? And certainly you didn't try the old pen and ink very often.

Well, Jimmy, old dear, I'll try to think kinder thoughts before long and wish you everything in your work.

Affectionately,

MARY

He read it over two or three times. There was no Mary in it. He couldn't recognize a single phrase. But perhaps women are like that: more fierce and relentless than men, when their minds are made up.

He rang Lamont's hotel. As he expected, he was no longer registered there; his luggage had been removed by Miss Lamont. Suddenly he realized that he lacked even a trace of her. She had melted out of his sight completely.

Gillespie was sure to find out before long. It was no surprise to Kildare when, late in the afternoon, Gillespie said: 'What's this about Mary Lamont giving up her job? To take care of her brother?'

'So it seems,' said Kildare.

'Seems? Don't you know?'

'No, sir.'

'Wait a minute. Where is the girl?'

'I don't know, sir.'

'You what?'

'I don't know, sir.'

'Well, I'll be damned,' said Gillespie. 'You mean that you're wrecked on this business of the brother?'

Kildare said nothing. For suddenly it seemed to him that there was no breath left in him for speech.

'You mean,' went on Gillespie, 'that you'll let her fade out of your life without making a single effort?'

'If I could find her ...' said Kildare. 'But New York's a big place.'

'Bah!' said Gillespie. 'If you gave a single damn about her, you'd track her down in five minutes.'

But the stream of the hospital work did not slacken, and Kildare was surprised to find himself seeing as clearly, thinking as swiftly as ever. Within him there was the persistent ache of his heart, but he was accustomed to that sort of pain. He had grown up familiar with it, when he was fighting his way through school.

Gillespie called in the ambulance driver, Joe Weyman.

He said: 'Weyman, you've got an eye in your head. Start using it. Mary Lamont has disappeared. Kildare can't find her. Your friend Mike Ryan knows the police. Ask him what to do. And get out in your infernal ambulance and start cruising like a taxicab. You might find out something. You know the sort of hotels she'd stop at, the sort of restaurants she'd eat in.'

'She left? *She* left the doc?' breathed Weyman.

Gillespie scowled.

'I've given you the facts. Go out and do something about them. I'll cover you on the use of the ambulance. Get going, Weyman!'

So Weyman got going, hurrying like a frightened animal to Mike Ryan, first of all.

Mike Ryan leaned his elbows on the edge of the bar and shook his head. 'It ain't likely to of happened,' said Mike. 'I've seen her and I've heard her talk. It ain't the sort of thing she'd do.'

'Yeah, but you never can tell with a gal that's had education mixed up in her head,' said Weyman.

'That's true,' agreed Ryan. 'You get a female that thinks she can think, and all hell is likely to pay for it. They get proud of their ideas. You can't never tell any man or any woman, either, when they start thinking their way out.'

'Get the cops on the job,' said Weyman. 'I'm gonna go cruising.'

So he went cruising, hour by hour, while

the day clouded over and the soft, slow rain began to fall. At fifty places he made his inquiries; but the day had ended and the twilight begun before he saw Mary Lamont beside a street lamp, seeing to the loading of luggage into a taxicab. By the time he had pulled in beside the curb, the girl was gone back into the little hotel.

'Hai, taxi,' said Weyman, 'where does *that* load go?'

'It's catching a boat for South America at seven o'clock,' said the taxi. 'Why?'

'What pier?' asked Weyman.

'Forty-three, I think,' said the taxi-driver. 'What's the idea, brother?'

Weyman, for answer, dropped his gear shift lever into first and made the engine howl as he shot the ambulance down the street. He had no time to spare. There would be a saving if he simply stopped and telephoned the news to the doc; but a telephone call was a dull way of doing something that could be made so dramatic.

He foretasted his hurried entry, his breathless rush into Kildare's office. Therefore, although the time was short to get to the hospital and leave the warning, he stepped on the gas and prepared his speech.

He was grinning so that he hardly saw the ten-year-old urchin that jumped out from the curb, laughing, his head turned to watch the running boy behind him. He was hardly ten feet away before Weyman snapped out of his day-dream and swerved the heavy ambulance.

The boy, screeching, jumped aside and missed death by a scant fraction; and on that street oiled by the rain the ambulance squirted sideways, out of control, like a wet watermelon seed shot out from between thumb and forefinger.

Weyman, desperately trying to right it, saw the rear of a great twenty-ton trailer-truck loom through the rain mist. The red of the rear-end lights streaked across his brain; then the crash blotted out the world.

When Joe Weyman came to, he felt nothing but a numbness. A policeman was kneeling beside him.

Someone said: 'They oughta shoot him; they oughta put him out of his misery. God, I never seen nothing like it!'

Weyman bent his head and saw that they were speaking of him. His body was like a hillside after a spring rain. Blood gushed from twenty small fountains. He tried to lift his hand and brush away some blood that was tickling his upper lip. But he could not move his hand. His legs were spread-eagled in a queer way that made no sense. They were not two legs. They were a jumble.

A siren came toward them, screaming.

'Take it easy, bucko,' said the policeman. 'There'll be a doctor here in a minute and slide a shot into you, and then you'll be all right. You won't feel nothing.'

'Wait a minute,' said Weyman. 'I gotta think. There was something that I had to do. I had to do something for the doc...'

'Leave the doc wait,' said the cop. 'Think about yourself, brother, for a while.'

'Listen, guy—officer, I mean—I'm cooked. I'm passing out. I can't only half see you. For God's sake have a heart and do what I ask. Will you?'

'I'll do it.'

'Get out your book.'

'I've got it out.'

'Write down—telephone board, Blair General Hospital, gal named Sally.'

'I've got it.'

'Never mind. Leave that till later. There's a doctor in that hospital ... Kildare.'

'Okay.'

'Grab a taxi and beat it for the hospital. Get to him. If you have to break down doors, get to him.'

'I'll get to him, all right,' said the officer.

'Tell him that Mary Lamont—L-A-M-O-N-T —leaving for South America. Pier...'

Darkness lifted suddenly above his lips, above his eyes. He heard a voice calling faintly to him: 'What pier, buddy?'

'Pier Forty-three. Seven o'clock. Tell Sally...'

CHAPTER EIGHTEEN

I'D HAVE A PRAYER

They brought Tim Creegan into the operating room at Blair General; and he was in a panic. The nurses were contemptuous.

'If you'd give me only half a second to see the doc,' whined Creegan.

'Hold up a minute,' said Bixby. 'What doc? Dr. Kildare?'

'Yeah, the doc,' said Creegan.

'I'll try to get him for you,' said Bixby. 'But he's a busy man, Creegan.'

'Yeah, but if I could just lay an eye on him for a minute, and hear him tell me it'll be all right.'

So Kildare came, hurrying.

'Simple appendectomy,' said Bixby. 'No signs of any complications. All clear sailing.'

'Doc,' said Creegan, 'is it true? Is it all right?'

'It's all right,' said Kildare.

'Are they gunna put me out, first? Are they gunna choke off my wind?'

'Did you give Creegan a good shot before you brought him in here?'

'I did,' said Bixby, 'but he's terribly nervous. It didn't seem to take the edge off him at all.'

162

'Doc, stand by a minute, will you?' begged Creegan. 'I can't breathe good.'

He struggled to sit upright.

'Steady,' said Kildare, and laid a hand on his arm.

Creegan lay like a stone, his eyes begging Kildare.

'Let me do this job, Bixby, will you?' asked Kildare.

'Why not?' said Bixby. 'I'll ring the office.'

'My God, doc,' said Creegan.

'It's going to be all right,' said Kildare.

'You mean you'll do the whole job with your own hands?'

'The whole job,' said Kildare.

'From first to last, and nobody else touch me?'

'Nobody else, Tim.'

'Love of God, it's more'n I could ask for ... Would somebody please tell Minnie, where she's waiting in the room, half wild, poor thing? Would somebody please to tell her that the doc is going to do it all with his own hands, and there's no worry no more?'

Someone left the room.

'Now,' said Kildare, nodding to the anaesthetician. 'Careful, please ... it's going to be easy, Tim ... First you'll feel a little shut off in the breathing, but keep on breathing slow and deep ... I'm right here. This is my hand on your head. I won't stir away till you're sound asleep, and you'll wake up better than new...'

There was not a stir from Creegan, only a deeply rumbled murmur of content.

After a while the great Gillespie came in, and the operating room drew to a fine tension under those all-seeing eyes.

'Not going so fast today, Jimmy, I see,' he said.

'No, sir,' said Kildare.

'Man has a belly like an ox!' said Gillespie. 'Plenty of bottom to *that* animal. Ten men like that could lift the Empire State Building...'

There was a slight confusion at the door. A nurse spoke to someone outside who insisted on coming in. Finally she returned with a slip of paper, deeply stained with red at one corner.

She said: 'A message for you, doctor.'

'Later on,' said Kildare.

'No, doctor. Now!' insisted the nurse.

He saw the bigness of her eyes through the white mask.

'Well?' he said, taking the paper.

'An officer brought it from Joe Weyman, the ambulance driver. He was hurt in an accident. And he gave the officer this message ... And he died, doctor.'

'Weyman? Dead?' said Kildare.

He took a deep breath, shrugged back his shoulders, and read the message.

Mary Lamont leaves Pier Forty-three at seven o'clock bound for South America.

He crumpled the paper and let it drop; then he leaned over the operation again. His hands were a little slower, but perfectly sure. Gillespie had caught the crumpled paper out of the air. He smoothed it.

'Hold on!' said Gillespie. 'Bixby, can't you take this over? There's a terribly important thing for Kildare to do.'

'I'm glad to take over,' said Bixby. 'Thanks, Jimmy. You just run along.'

'I promised him,' said Kildare through his teeth.

'You fool!' cried Gillespie. 'There's not twenty minutes before the sailing. If you miss her now, you've missed her forever. And what's Creegan but a human ox, anyway?'

'I promised him,' said Kildare. 'From the first touch to the last stitch, it's to be all my work.'

'Then, by God, you're right,' said Gillespie. He whirled the wheelchair around.

'Open that door—and get out of my way!' he ordered.

*   *   *

The last visitors were off the *Caballero* when a man in white was pushed up the gangway by a second white-clad figure. The second

165

officer met them at the head of the gangplank.

'Entirely too late for visitors, sir,' he said.

'It's not too late for me. I'm not a visitor,' said Gillespie.

'What is this all about, sir?' asked the officer.

'It's a melodrama,' said Gillespie. 'There's gold in them hills; and there's a girl in the hands of Indians—and you're the Indians, brother. And I'm the United States cavalry to the rescue. Get passenger Mary Lamont up here to me, and get her fast!'

'It's Dr. Gillespie, of the Blair General Hospital; it's the great Gillespie himself,' the ambulance driver was explaining to the purser of the little ship.

A moment later Mary Lamont was brought into the purser's office and faced the belligerent stare of Gillespie.

'Leave us alone,' said Gillespie, to the ship's officer. 'Now, Mary, what hellish contraption are you up to now?'

'I'm taking my brother to a place where he can have quiet and a change,' she said.

'And leaving Kildare in hell about you, eh?'

'If I've upset him a little, he'll soon be all right,' she said.

'Fallen out of love, have you?'

'I'm sorry, doctor.'

'Cool about it all, ain't you?'

166

'We weren't right for one another. It's much better this way,' she said.

'He don't amount to much in your eyes, it seems?'

'I'm afraid not, doctor,' she said.

'Why, what a little tin-whistle, penny-a-dozen liar you turn out to be!' said Gillespie. 'Get down on your knees and ask God Almighty to forgive you for being such a liar!'

'I'm not lying, doctor,' she said.

'You are! You're lying, and lying and lying in every line of your little wooden, white face. Why do you keep your hand over your heart, except that the thought of Kildare is killing you every minute?'

'No, doctor,' she said.

'Don't "no doctor" me, either. Do you think that you can fool me, you empty-headed little rattle-trap? Do you think that I don't know you like a book? Yes, a first grade reader. Words of one syllable. That's how simple you are to me.'

'Doctor Gillespie, I'm sorry that you're wrong.'

'Sorry, are you? I'll make you a damned sight sorrier. Pull that chair over here beside me ... Now sit down in it ... Now put your head on my shoulder.'

He pulled her forcefully down to him.

'Now cry, you little fool!' said Gillespie. 'You're not right for one another, eh? It's better this way, is it?'

She began to tremble. She clutched her face with both hands, but the tears forced through.

There was a strong knocking at the door.

'The ship sails in five minutes!' called the purser.

'Get the luggage of Mary Lamont and her brother on shore,' said Gillespie. 'Get it right out on the dock, or I'll make you wish that you had yellow fever on board instead of me!'

'I can't go back to him,' whispered Mary.

'Can't you? You're not going back. You're being carried back, and I'm the one that's doing the carrying.'

'You don't know—oh, you don't know!' she gasped. 'It isn't only the one stain in my family's blood. There are two. I can't marry Jimmy. I can't marry him, I can't. I can't have children. There was another dreadful case...'

Her hand instinctively found the second letter from her cousin. It had arrived only that day and she exposed the moist twist of it inside the handkerchief which she carried.

'There was my poor uncle. He died in an institution in Peoria. And now there's Douglas—and I don't even dare think of marriage, and the curse I could bring to poor Jimmy's life!'

'What are you talking about?' said Gillespie. 'There's no "institution" for the insane in Peoria; but there's a poorhouse there. Is that what you're talking about? And as for the epilepsy, it's no more hereditary than measles, you little ramping, raving idiot! Not if there were ten cases in ten generations; it wouldn't mean a damned thing more than chance!'

'That isn't true!' whispered the girl. She slipped out of the chair onto her knees. She held one of Gillespie's old, tough hands between hers. 'It isn't true. You're only making me crazy with happiness!'

'You'll be a damned sight crazier, then, when Kildare gets through with you.'

They got Douglas Lamont to bed in the hospital. 'Where I can watch his regime myself,' said Gillespie, 'because he belongs to you, and you to Jimmy, and Jimmy to me; so the whole damned tribe of you are in my pocket, where I intend to keep you till I'm satisfied. The whole damned kit and caboodle,' said Gillespie. 'Now we'll find Jimmy.'

'Not yet,' said Mary. 'I'm going to ask Miss Cavendish, first, if she'll permit me to return to the hospital and then—'

'I'll attend to that Cavendish woman,' said the terrible Gillespie. 'You come with me and face the music.'

So she had to go with him in the elevator down to the first floor. And there, in the hallway, they met Jimmy face to face, walking slowly, with the arm of little Sally, the telephone operator, drawn through his. And she, from the turn of her bowed head toward him, seemed still to be weeping.

He did not see them, so great was his preoccupation in Sally. They could not make out his words, but the gentle murmur of his voice was giving infinite comfort.

'Steady, steady, Mary,' said Gillespie, as the two disappeared around a bend in the corridor. 'Did you see what I saw? *Her* man is dead, Mary ... Medicine, surgery, panaceas—if I were a boy again, I'd make a new start all over again, and do you know what I'd do, my dear girl? I'd learn how to pray. I'd learn one damned good prayer and have it ready when the time comes that nothing else can help.'

Max Brand is the best-known pen name of Frederick Faust, creator of Dr. Kildare, Destry, and many other fictional characters popular with readers and viewers worldwide. Faust wrote for a variety of audiences in many genres. His enormous output, totalling approximately thirty million words or the equivalent of 530 ordinary books, covered nearly every field: crime, fantasy, historical romance, espionage, Westerns, science fiction, adventure, animal stories, love, war, and fashionable society, big business and big medicine. Eighty motion pictures have been based on his work along with many radio and television programs. For good measure he also published four volumes of poetry. Perhaps no other author has reached more people in more different ways.

Born in Seattle in 1892, orphaned early, Faust grew up in the rural San Joaquin Valley of California. At Berkeley he became a student rebel and one-man literary movement, contributing prodigiously to all campus publications. Denied a degree because of unconventional conduct, he embarked on a series of adventures culminating in New York City where, after a period of near starvation, he received simultaneous recognition as a serious poet and successful popular-prose writer. Later, he travelled widely, making his home in New York, then in Florence, and finally in Los Angeles.

Once the United States entered the Second World War, Faust abandoned his lucrative writing career and his work as a screenwriter to serve as a war correspondent with the infantry in Italy, despite his fifty-one years and a bad heart. He was killed during a night attack on a hilltop village held by the German army. New books based on magazine serials or unpublished manuscripts continue to appear. Alive and dead he has averaged a new one every four months for seventy-five years. In the U.S. alone nine publishers issue his work, plus many more in foreign countries. Yet, only recently have the full dimensions of this extraordinarily versatile and prolific writer come to be recognized and his stature as a protean literary figure in the 20th Century acknowledged. His popularity continues to grow throughout the world.